RANDAL

CALHOUN MEN BOOK 5

KATHI S. BARTON

This is a work of fiction. Names, characters, places, and incidents are products of the author's imagination or are used fictitiously and are not to be construed as real. Any resemblance to actual events, locations, organizations, or persons, living or dead, is entirely coincidental.

World Castle Publishing, LLC
Pensacola, Florida
Copyright © Kathi S. Barton 2017
Paperback ISBN: 9781629898124
eBook ISBN: 9781629898131
First Edition World Castle Publishing, LLC, October 16, 2017
http://www.worldcastlepublishing.com
Cover: Karen Fuller
Editor: Maxine Bringenberg

Chapter 1

Randal had forty-three bags filled with enough food for the kids to take home. There were extras—he only had a class of twenty-four—but he knew that some of the kids, a lot of them as a matter of fact, had siblings at home, and he wanted to make sure there was enough for all of them. He looked over at his helper and smiled. Heather was having fun helping him, he thought.

"Mr. Randal, when we get done here, can I go with you to hand them out?" He told her that was all right with him. "I know that Mark has no food right now, and his power has been off. They didn't have the money for bills this time."

It was getting better in town. The new plant was hiring more all the time. And even though there were faeries and brownies around to help with the cleaning, he had hired about fifty of the elderly to do it as well. It was working out for a great many people, the jobs as well as the influx of money to the local stores. But as Heather pointed out, some people were still having troubles, and some of them were just not going to help themselves. And as such, he'd only go so far in his help to them.

"We'll give him two bags for his home, all right?" She nodded and grinned at him. "You're a good friend of his, so you tell him that if he gets hungry again before the break is over, to call us. Okay?"

"Yes. I can do that. But he'll have to see me in town. He don't have a phone either." He corrected her. "He doesn't have a phone either."

"My goodness, look at what you two have been doing." It was two days before Christmas and his grandda had been as jolly as he'd ever seen him. When he asked if he could help out, Heather ran to him, giving the old man a hug and kiss. "I heard that you would need a truck to deliver things in. I brought my old beater for us."

"Thanks, Grandda." They loaded the bags of food into the truck and then in his Jeep when they had filled the truck. Grandma and his mom showed up about the time they were ready to head out. "You come to help out?"

"Yes, and we have gift cards too." He wasn't sure about that and he told his mom that. "You just leave that to me, son. Some of these people are doing without, and we've devised a way to make it a merrier Christmas for a lot of them."

His grandma rode with Grandda, and his mom with him and Heather. The first house they stopped at was little Mark's. His cheeks were rosy from the cold, and that was inside the house. But carrying the bags of food inside, he noticed something else. They weren't going to make it on the little that he'd brought them, and he looked at his mom when she cleared her throat.

"Mr. Dennis. The power company will be out in an hour or less to turn your heat and electric back on." The lights flickered then came on just as his mom finished talking. "Very nice. Now, here are some gift cards for you. You're to take them to the store that is on the card, and they have a nice filled bag for you and your children. Also, we've set up a sitter for you when you're off, as well as a car for you to use to find you a job at the new plant. I have to insist that you go there and do that, Mr. Dennis. These children cannot make it on their own if you're taken to jail. Don't you think?"

"Yes, ma'am. You're right. I've been...it's been hard here without the missus, and without them being at school all day, I don't have anyone to watch over them. But with this, I don't know what to say. Since my wife passed, it's been so hard on us. I don't want to be on charity, but we're hurting mightily bad here." His mom hugged the younger man and then held him while he sobbed about how he appreciated what was being done for them. "We didn't have anything for dinner tonight until you showed up."

Randall went to this car and brought in two more of the bags of food, and heard his mom telling Mr. Dennis that there would be more in the coming days as well. When they left, Heather looked up at him with a huge smile.

"You're nice. I know that all the time, but you made them happy." He picked her up and told her that was what families did, help someone that needed it. "My mom and dad didn't. They only helped each other. I miss them sometimes, but not a lot. When is my aunt coming here?"

"Today." Randal put her in the booster seat. Not because she was young enough to need it, but she was underweight and couldn't be without one until she gained a few more pounds. It had broken his heart the first time they ate together.

She'd asked him if she could have some extra wrap. It took

his mind a couple of seconds to figure out what she meant when Wally, his new cook, told her that whenever she needed food, that she was to come to him. Apparently she was going to wrap up what she'd not been able to eat to save for when she was alone again. Which was never going to happen, as far as he was concerned.

Laney Price was supposed to be at the house in an hour. Not his; she was staying with his brother, Sterl, and Marty, his wife. There were things going on regarding Laney that worried him. For one thing, he had a feeling that Laney was going to be his mate. He had no idea why he thought so, but he just knew that having this little girl in his life was going to bring him a whole new set of issues. Not bad ones, just things he'd have to take care of.

He got home later that night, exhausted but feeling pretty good about things when he walked around his home. It was a nice one, yes, but needed a great deal of work. Siting in the living room with nothing more than a chair and a small television, he reached out for Myra, the witch who had become a good friend of his. And when she appeared in his living room with him, he smiled. There was always something to smile about when she came to visit him. Whether it was for business or pleasure, she was a delight to him.

"Hello, my dear. How are you making it?" He laughed, then told her his thoughts. "For you, in the event that you didn't know, I'd do anything. You're a good boy...all of you are, but you are special to me."

Her costume, because that was how he thought of them, was book covers. The titles of them, and the authors, were some of his favorites. Even her hair had some printed covers on it, and he got up to look them over. She was a treat, Myra was, and had she been anyone else, he would've thought she was flirting with him every time she was around.

"I was wondering what I'd have to repay you with if you were to finish my home. I think, but I'm not sure, that my mate is on her way here, and I want to have things ready for her." She sat down and he joined her on the nice couch that hadn't been there before. His had been old and ratty; this one was new and softer than warm butter. "You know this house as well as I do, I think. But it needs to be done. Not just with me in mind, but her as well."

"You are much smarter than I thought, and I already knew you were brilliant. I know the woman coming too. She is going to give you a hard time, just so you know." He said that he'd not have it any other way. "Good boy. Now, I can only do so much to this house without her impressions of it. She has been without for far too long for you to just give her it all at once. You'll overwhelm and frighten her a great deal if you do."

"I understand. She is aware of us, I think, correct?" Myra said that she knew of shifters, but not what they were. "Okay. I guess that's good and bad. When she arrives, what do you think I should do?"

"Be yourself. You are a charmer when it comes to that. And smart when it comes to women. Of all the Calhoun men, I think that you've had less experience with good women than you have bad ones, but you're going to be fine. If you listen with your head as well as your heart."

He nodded, but didn't move. Randal did want to ask her questions, but he was sure that he'd not get any answers to them. This was, if she was his mate, up to him. And with what Myra had said, he was sure of it. He looked around the living room and noticed while he'd been thinking, the room had shifted and was dressed. Randal had called a room being finished and ready for people dressed since he'd become a teacher. He loved dressing his room for the new school year.

"Your home, like those of your brothers, is magical now. I think you will need it." He asked her if bad was coming their way. "Yes. I cannot tell you what it is, but you will be fine if you listen. Not just to your mate, but to your family as well. I think it's been pointed out to you before that you are the most trusting of all of them."

"Yes, and while it burns me a little to think I was so easily pegged, I've come to realize that I'm all right with it. But I have taken precautions so that no one thinks that after they try something." She told him he was clever, and it wouldn't hurt him to be prepared at his school too. "I am."

Something occurred to him then, a thought that he didn't much care for. But before he could ask her about it, the doorbell rang. He made his way to it, thinking that it was mighty late for someone to be coming around in a snowstorm. When he looked out the little glass on the door, he looked at Myra.

"Should I be worried?" She nodded, then shook her head. He noticed that she'd changed. That now she was dressed entirely in Christmas decorations. Even small trees hung from her ears. "You're not very helpful, are you?"

"It will not harm you, but you should guard your heart." He wasn't sure if she meant literally or figuratively, and didn't get the chance to ask before she disappeared. Randal looked out the glass again and then opened it slowly.

"Can I help you?" The man standing there wasn't anyone that he knew. Nor did he think it was anyone his family might know. He turned away from Randal then, and he noticed that there was a woman on the lawn. It was Mrs. Watson, Billy Watson's mom. "What's this about?"

"You think we need your charity?" Randal said nothing but did reach for his brother, Scott, who he knew was with his wife Chloe, the chief of police. "You come into my house and give them food like we got nothing? You bastard. I got money enough for my shit."

"I didn't give it to just you, Mr. Watson, but that was the Christmas gift that I gave all my students. It was something I do every year." He asked him again if he'd thought he needed charity. "It's not charity, it's a gift. Would you like to come into my house? Mrs. Watson looks to be cold."

The man went to his wife and Randal watched him to make sure that he didn't hurt her. When he wrapped his arms around her and helped her into the house, he felt better, though he didn't call off his family yet, but he did feel better about it.

"I told you to stay in the car." Mrs. Watson shivered and wrapped the blanket that had been on the back of the couch around her. "Thank you, sir. I'm surely sorry about this, but I got my dander up."

"Understandable." When they were seated in this living room with the roaring fire, he thought of what Myra had warned him about when Mr. Watson stood up and drew a gun. "You're still mad."

"Of course I am. What right did you have thinking that any of them kids needed you to step in and bring them food? You think we're all a lazy bunch that needs the charity of an upstart like you? I told her that you were an uppity bastard when you bought some of them kids in your class their supplies. You and your family, you just loving rubbing it in

11

that we're all poorer than you, don't you?" Randal told his brother to hurry and why. "You got nothing to say?"

"Oh, I have plenty to say, but I don't think you're going to listen so I'm not going to waste my breath. But I have called the police as well as my family in." Mr. Watson told him that he'd done no such thing. "You go on believing that while you have a gun pointed at me for no other reason than you think I'm doing you wrong."

"Sit down." He nodded and made his way to the living room again, making sure that he left the front door not only unlocked but open just a little as well. He wasn't thrilled about having anyone hurt in his house, but he did make sure that if need be, someone could come in and save him. Randal wasn't macho enough to think that he could do this on his own.

There were places to hide in his house. When he'd taken it from Chloe, she'd shown him the panic room as well as the other features that her dad had put in to keep the people there safe. But the kitchen was too far away, and he didn't think he could outrun a bullet. Because as surely as he was sitting there, he knew this man had a plan.

~~~

"We have to make a stop." Laney was tossed to the side of the car when Sterl made a U-turn in the middle of the street. "My brother has a visitor that isn't being nice. We just want to make sure that he's all right before we take you to our house."

She'd read a great deal about the family before coming out here with these two. They were wealthy. And had she not just spent the last two hours with them, she might have thought them snobbish. But these two were far from it. Laney had learned a great deal from them too.

They were wolves. Both of them were shifters. And while

12

she wasn't afraid of them, she did have her moments of fear when she was around others like them. Laney had even told them about the guy at work who took great pleasure in chasing her around the parking lot when she got off work. The fucker knew better than to mess with her now…shooting at him with her small gun had stopped that sort of playing around, but he hadn't stopped threatening her.

The house that they pulled up in front of had several police cruisers in front, as well as a couple of cars. She stayed back when asked to, but watched what was going on. Whatever it was, the three men standing to the side of the house were pissed off, and she knew at once they were brothers to Sterl. They looked a great deal alike. Then the elderly man got out of his car and she laughed. Christ, they were like clones of him. Then she saw her stepsister.

Heather had been so tiny when she'd seen her the last time. An infant, she guessed now. But she held onto the hand of the woman that had been with the older man like she was never going to let her go. Laney felt her heart take a hard twist in her chest when she realized that she didn't know her.

"You should go and see her." Laney didn't look at Marty, but did shake her head. "Mom told me that she talks of nothing else but you coming to see her. I think it would do her and you a world of good to be together right now."

"I don't know why…she doesn't know me any more than I know her." Marty told her that they were family and that was all that mattered. "We don't have any sort of relationship. Not even a little one. I sent her cards when she was younger… not that she's old now, but I knew that my sister and her deadbeat husband were using the money for other things. So I stopped."

13

The little girl turned to see her and let go of the woman's hand to run to her. Laney scooped her up into her arms, forgetting all about her resolve to not let her get into her heart. Heather made her way there all on her own.

After kissing each other several times — it still didn't seem like enough — Laney hugged her. It had been as if the years had never happened, that they'd been together all this time. And when Heather told her, over and over, how much she had missed her, Laney cried with her, telling her how much she had missed her as well. She supposed that it was true that blood was thicker than water and tighter than a snare on a drum.

"Mr. Randal and his mom are taking good care of me. I have food all the time and a bed. It has so many blankets on it that I get lost sometimes." Laney told her she was sorry. "No, don't be, Aunt Laney. I like them. They're very soft and warm. Did you know that Mom and Dad are gone?"

"Yes, that's why I'm here. I've come to see about your welfare." She looked confused. "To make sure that you're all right and that you do have enough to eat, and blankets."

"I do. I love it here. You should see the Christmas trees that are in the houses. They're bigger than all of us." Which wasn't saying much. For a six-year-old, Heather was tall like her, but not big compared to the men that were walking toward them. "The Calhouns, they're my new uncles. I can call them that because they said I could. And I call Grandma, Grandma too."

She tried telling herself that she wasn't jealous of the men and women in Heather's life now. Laney knew that a big part of it was her own fault. She had distanced herself from them all. But it was do that and survive with her dignity and her life, or be sucked into their hell right along with her dad and sister. Laney knew that she would have not only been broke, but broken as well.

When the younger version of the man that had been with Heather came out, she felt her heart beating a little faster and her body warming. The instinct to go to him and see if he was all right startled her. The blood, she told herself…it was the blood all over his front and face that had warranted such a response from her. When Heather struggled to be put down she let her go, but watched her as she ran to the man.

They talked, the man kneeling down to her level so that he could let her touch him. Comfort…Heather was offering him comfort, even though she was much smaller than him and he was covered in blood. Making her way to the porch where the man was, she was shocked to see how tall he was. About five or so inches taller than her own six-foot frame.

"Hello." She nodded at his greeting. "Not the way I would have welcomed you here, but I'm glad that you made it safely."

"What a strange thing to say." The elderly couple just laughed, and she had a feeling that she wasn't in on a joke, or whatever it was they were making fun about. Laney was tired and she was also stressed, and when she was, her temper flared up. "My sister and I, we're grateful for all that you've done for us, and if you don't mind, I'd like to get back. A hotel would suit us better, I think."

"If you think so." She wasn't sure why he was grinning at her the way he was, but she didn't care for it, or the looks of the others. "I wanted to be the first to warn you that your father and stepmother are on their way here. I think they have it in their head to take Heather back with them. I'm glad that

15

you're aware that she's your sister and not your niece, but they're coming and I want you to be safe. We all do."

She turned to look at him when she started for the car. "Who told them that I was here? Did you? Was it in order to make me pay for something that they've done?"

"No. I don't know what they were told about your sister, only that she had passed. The next of kin was notified, and that was the number that the police had. I'm sure had they known about them, they would have made every effort to call you instead." He sat down; more like he fell down to the steps that led up to his porch. "I'm sorry. I've been.... I've had a stressful few minutes here. But I didn't know to notify them, and I wouldn't have anyway. I have no idea why, but I figured that you'd be better at taking care of Heather than them any day of the week. Was I right?"

"Yes. My stepmother...Rosemarie, she's not a nice person." Laney glanced at Heather, who was with the Calhouns again. "My stepmother, Sally Anne's biological mother, has been a bad influence on my sister all her life. And my father, my biological father, isn't much better. If they get Heather, even for a night, they'll hurt her and bury her someplace that no one will be able to find, just to take the money that might come to her. I don't know why I believe that, but I do."

"I figured as much too. We have some connections that have had their lives looked into. Also, you should know that the FBI is out looking for them too. Not in any kind of hurry, mind you, but they're here so that when they arrive, they'll be watched better than the locals can do. Just to make sure that when they do take them in, it'll stick." She asked what they had done just as someone handed him an ice bag. "Other than some of the outstanding bills they have at home, in their state, there is also the fact that they've been filing a tax return with the little girl's name on it as their child."

"She is their child." He nodded and it occurred to her what he meant. "My sister was doing the same thing with Heather."

"Yes."

He told her he was sorry and got up and ran into the house. She wasn't sure what had happened but she followed. As soon as she entered the house, she knew that this was a home made for a family. It was soft and soothing, the paint on the walls, the decorations in the rooms that she could see.

Laney heard him in the bathroom, throwing up. Knocking once on the door, she asked him if he was all right. His garbled answer didn't satisfy her since he threw up several more times, so she opened the door. The man was a mess, and his head leaning into the commode didn't do much for him at the moment. When he looked at her, his face pale and sort of green, she handed him a towel and sat on the little chair that was sitting there.

Trent, she thought his name was, as well as Sterl came by the little room to see if he was all right. When he didn't toss up his cookies anymore and sat on the floor, she thought he might make it. When the other two men left them, she asked him if he was really all right.

"I'm not sure. Have you ever been shot at?" She nodded at him. "I have too, but tonight was...he wanted to kill me because I had the nerve to help him out with a few extra groceries at his home over the holidays."

"Some people I know, most of them, either want more than you give them or they don't care to be labeled. I know what you were doing, but perhaps you might have made him feel bad for it." He said he'd figured that out about the time he'd shot him. "You were actually shot? Where? Has anyone looked at it?"

She tore at his shirt when he pointed to his shoulder. There was a small wound there, but for some reason she was positive that it had been worse before. When he put his hand over hers, she looked into his eyes.

"I'm going to be all right." She nodded and continued to stare at him. "You're really very beautiful. I know that I'm rushing things here, but can you kiss me? No, never mind. I wouldn't want to kiss me either. Not after this."

"Why not?" She realized that she was somewhat disappointed and pushed herself up to her feet. "I'm sorry that you're hurt, but I really have to be going now. My sister and I, I think we've taken up enough of your family's time."

She was out the door and into the car in seconds. If anyone spoke to her, she didn't know what they might have said on her flight to the car she'd come here in. Heather joined her a few minutes later, then the Calhouns. Laney thought the faster she got home the better. Something was really strange here, and it was affecting her too.

CHAPTER 2

Randal was just putting the last few entries in his January school newsletter when he realized how late it was. He was supposed to be at his parents' house in an hour, and he still had to shovel off the driveway and drive over. Walking sounded good – he didn't have to go anywhere else afterwards – and he decided that he'd be better off leaving now rather than later.

Going to his deck, he saw them before they noticed him. Laney had grown up in a very hot place, while her sister had been in Ohio her entire life. He could see the difference in the way they were dressed, how much one of them was prepared for it and the other was clueless. He whistled loudly, getting both their attention before Heather waved at him and started toward his home. Laney seemed to be torn over whether to come or go.

"I have a fire in the fireplace, and can have hot cocoa and cookies ready before you get here." That decided her and she came at him. When she fell the third time, having no idea how to walk in the snow, he made his way toward her. "Come on, darling. Let me help you."

"Aren't you cold?" Her teeth were chattering now and her fingers were ice cold. "This is the worst weather I've ever had the misfortune of being in. I hate the cold."

"This is nothing. Wait until January when it really snows." She stopped walking and he laughed. "You'll get used to it, I think. Heather and I have built several snowmen over the last couple of weeks."

"Why are you here?" He said that he lived here. "No, I mean, on this property. I thought your dad said it belonged to him."

"No, I have a few hundred acres, as well as a pond in the back that is perfect for skating on this time of year. And swimming, I guess, in the summer. I've not lived here that long yet." She asked him if he was serious. "Yes. I got the house from Chloe when she settled up her dad's estate a few weeks back. I'd been working on it, but had someone come in and finish things up for me before you arrived."

They were on the deck now, and he helped brush the snow off her. Heather was inside, no doubt asking Wally for seconds by now. When they entered the house, he noticed that not only was there a fire in the hearth, but also a warm looking blanket on the couch. He helped Laney to it and covered her up.

"You should take off your boots." She told him she was sorry for tracking snow in. "No, that's fine, but you'll warm up faster if you take them off. They're wet through."

"I didn't have any idea what sort of weather there was out here. I mean, I knew it was cold and all, but not this much snow. I've been skiing, once, but it was manmade snow, not this kind." Randal pulled off her boots and set them by the fireplace. He knew that they'd be dry in no time; the magic of the house would take care of them both now. "Did you really have hot cocoa, or were you just trying to entice me into the house?"

"Both. And Wally is good at reading your mind." She only stared at him when the man himself came into the room with a tray containing not only a pitcher of cocoa, but also a plate of cookies and scones. Heather was close behind him.

"I like your house now, Mr. Randal. It's way better than it was last week. Did you call someone in to help you?" He smiled and winked at Heather. "You should have seen this place before, Aunt Laney. He had like a million projects going at one time. And they were never going to get done."

"Heather, that's not nice." She laughed and told her sister that was what he'd said. "Not the handyman type, are you?"

"No, not really. I would rather pay someone to come in and do the work rather than try and figure it out on my own. I could, I guess. I worked with my grandda when I was in college as he renovated a lot of homes in the pack. But it wasn't something that I ever enjoyed."

"What did my sister mean when she said that this house looked better? The reason I ask is, I've been staying with your brother and sister-in-law, and their rooms move." Randal told her that they all did. "I see. And this thing that it does…I'm guessing that it's not anything you do?"

"Yes and no." Heather asked if she could have a snack and Wally said he'd make sure that she ate a good one. When she left the two of them alone and followed who she only assumed was Wally the mind reader, Randal moved to sit on the couch with her. "The house finds what you like by searching your mind, and makes the adjustment to suit it.

21

Enlarging the room, should you need it. Even the furniture could be made more accommodating. Like this couch. When I came in here today, there wasn't a nice new couch here, it was ratty and old. You liked this couch better, and the house provided it."

"You expect me to believe that?" He just shrugged at her. "I don't, and I don't think it's very nice of you to say something like that."

"Ah, I see." Laney asked him what it was he thought he saw. "You had this room in mind, and are now pissed that it looks like what you imagined. I'm guessing you think I did this somehow."

"No. Yes. I don't know." She put her hand over her eyes and sat there. The room took on another change and he laughed. When she looked around, he waited for her to say something. But all she did was stare at the mantel over the fireplace. "That wasn't there before."

"Yes, I'm aware of that." He got up and pulled the pottery vase off the mantel and looked at it. "This is very beautiful. And I think you should have more thoughts like this. I love this room."

"You can't be serious." He sat back down after putting the vase back. "That same vase is at my apartment. I don't know what's going on."

"I told you." He felt the touch of magic and knew who it was. Myra said she'd be by to meet his mate, so he looked at Laney. "There is a friend of the family that will be here shortly. I'm only telling you this because she can be blunt and outlandish. I love her to pieces, and she's the one that helped me with the magic of getting the house ready for you."

"Why me?" Myra came into the room. Not walked,

though he wished that she had, but just appeared. Laney gave a short scream, but didn't run like he might have seeing Myra dressed as she was today. "That is quite the outfit. Where are on earth did you get that? I'm assuming that you paid money for it?"

"Never. My goodness, you're more beautiful than I thought you'd be." As she was sitting down, her purple outfit became less colorful but no less bizarre. The paisley that she wore right now reminded him of another of her outfits that she'd had on, and he laughed a little. "I love color. And someone, I won't name who it was, pointed out that my color matched my mood. I have since given it a great deal of thought, and decided that I was going to be more of a challenge in making people aware of me when I enter a room. But I make them magically, I don't buy them. How are you enjoying your stay, Laney?"

"I'm not sure yet. It's very cold here, and I have a feeling that when I go back to Vegas, it's going to seem three times hotter." Myra looked at him and so did Laney. "Did I miss something here?"

"You've not told her then?" Randal shook his head and explained that he'd not wanted her to be upset. "She is now."

"Yes, I thank you for that." Laney looked at him and asked him what was going on. "I'm your mate, your other half."

"No." She stood up and he did as well. "I knew there was a trick to me coming out here. No one is that generous with their plane and shit. When can I go? Your brother assured me that I'd be able to leave as soon as I wanted. And don't even think about begging me to stay here. I have nothing here I want but my sister."

"You can go now, if you'd like. I can have the jet ready

whenever you're ready." She nodded and he watched her. "But, you should know that I'm going with you. I'm not going to beg you to stay, I'd never do that. But where you go, I will."

She looked at Myra then back at him. Randal thought that she was holding onto her temper very well. He might have exploded by now. But instead of saying anything else to upset her, he asked her to have a seat and let Myra explain a few things.

"I don't need anyone explaining to me what a mate means. I'm not stupid." Randal told her that he didn't believe that she was. "And I'm not going to be your bedmate, nor am I going to be at your beck and call."

"I should hope not." She looked at him, confused. "If you'd just have a seat, I'm sure that Myra can explain a great deal to you. I asked her to look into a few things for me, and she might have some information that we can use. Please?"

He was sure she was going to bolt. Randal wasn't worried that he'd not be able to go with her, but he didn't want to leave. He had a good job, a nice house now, and his family was here. But she was his world now, and he wasn't going to be without her. When she finally sat down he did as well, but at a distance. Spooking her was the last thing he wanted to do.

"Very well, I'm Myra. I have no last name. I never cared for adopting one, so I didn't. I'm the second hand to the queen White Witch. Her name is Chris Bentley. Such a lovely young woman, and so full of magic that it—" Randal cleared his throat. "Yes. I'm sorry. I get sidetracked sometimes. Anyway, your parents. I've had a faerie and a brownie watching over them for the last few days. My goodness, they are a pair, aren't they?"

"You have no idea. What sort of things have they been

doing? I'm aware that they know of my sister's death." Myra said that they'd been made aware the day that it happened. "And how are they taking it? I'm assuming that they're coming here for some reason."

"Yes, to take the child. They have been taking a great deal of funds from the community that they live in. I don't mean that things have been donated to them and that's how they got them, but they've been stealing things too. I would imagine, as good as they've become at it, that they've been doing it for some time." Laney said ever since they'd been married. "Yes, well that explains a great deal. I hope you don't mind, my dear, but I've slowed them down a bit. A little magic here and there and it'll take them a little longer than they had hoped to come to this town. Nothing to harm them, though I think they might deserve it, but just a flat tire and a little engine trouble. That's all."

"Why are you doing this for me? Or is it for him?" She nodded at him and he thought of how much he liked her having all the information up front like this. It was better for them all. When she glared at him again, he laughed. "I'm not sure I like you at the moment, so back off."

"You like me, admit it." She glared and he laughed harder. "You're very adorable when you're pissed off. Did you —? Fuck, that hurt."

She'd pinched him. And hard. He'd bet anything that he'd have a bruise on his belly in a few minutes. But in an hour, less probably, it would be gone. Still, she had spunk… that was all he could think about.

"I've also come to tell you, so that you're not left in the dark, as to what you've gained by being Randal's mate." Laney said that she wasn't. "But you are. And as such, you have

25

gained a great deal of magic. So has your sister, Heather. She will need it, I'm afraid, as will you. You are both immortal."

~~~

Laney knew that she should be packing. Or something. But she just couldn't get her head into it. The words, some of them as nutty as the woman seemed to be, kept circling around in her head like an embroidery hoop. Not that she sewed that much, but Laney did know what that was.

Heather came in to sit with her. "You okay?" She said that she was thinking. "Are you mad at me? I didn't want to go into their room, but I was very hungry and Dad had all the money in his pants."

She'd been told by Sterl that Heather had lived with her dead sister and brother-in-law for a long time. And that she'd taken money from Clay's wallet to buy some food. It broke her heart to know what she'd gone through. And she also knew there was going to be more to come with her dad and stepmother coming, but they'd deal with them when they arrived.

"No, I could never be mad at you, Heather. Why would you think that?" She shrugged, a habit that Laney figured out she did when she was afraid someone might not like her answer. "I have to tell you a few things. I don't know if you'll understand them or not, but you need to be aware of them."

"You mean that you're not my aunt? I know that, silly." Laney asked her who had told her, thinking that it had to be one of the Calhouns. "Mom did. Well, she's my sister too. She told me. But she told me to never tell anyone. She said that my check would go away. I don't know what that means, but she never told me a secret before."

"I would imagine that she had a lot of secrets. And I'm

sorry that you were so hungry." She said it was all right. She wasn't hungry any more. "Yes. When we go back to my place, I'll make sure you have lots to eat too."

"Are we going to pack up your things to come back?" Laney told her that they'd not be coming back. "But why? I like it here. I have my friends and my school. I can't go out there with you. What will I do with my stuff?"

"Honey, I don't live here. I have a job and everything out west. You'll love it out there. It never snows and it's always warm. We have a pool too that you can use." She said that there was one here for her. "Yes, but I don't live here. Don't you see? We have to go back there. I have a life there, and you're going to be a part of it."

"I don't want to be a part of it if I have to move. I don't like you." It cut her deeply to have her sister say that, but when someone told her to stop that, they both looked at the doorway. "She said that I have to move out there with her."

Randal looked at her and she could see that he was upset. At her or her sister, she wasn't sure, but she lifted her chin to show him that she didn't care. For some reason, she felt like a fool in front of him, and she hurt too.

"Is that the way we treat someone, Heather? Do we tell tales about how we feel about them just because something doesn't go our way?" She bowed her head and spoke, but Randal wasn't having any of it. "Look at me when I'm addressing you. You hurt your sister. How would you feel if my mom or my dad said that to you?"

She looked at Randal with something Laney had never seen on her face before...respect and love. Things that Heather had never had for her since she'd been there. Heather tolerated her, but she didn't look at her as she did this man.

27

"They love me." Randal told Heather that Laney did as well. "Then why is she making me go away from here? I love the snow and the pool. I have food all the time here, and someone that hugs me. I never got to hug anyone but you when my mom was here. Now she wants to take it all from me. 'Cause she's got a life out there."

"What do you think would have happened to you should your mother and father be here with you?" She bowed her head again, but lifted it when he asked her again. "Do you think that they'd be making sure you had food in your belly? That you had a warm bed when you went to sleep? How about a coat or a Christmas tree? Do you think that they would have given you those things?"

"No. They didn't like me." Laney started to tell her sister that they loved her, but she didn't when Randal asked her if she thought her sister loved her. "Yes. She does. But I still don't want to move."

"Perhaps you don't. But you have to have someone caring for you that loves you. And I'm sure that your sister will provide those things and more for you if you have to go. Now, I have to talk to your sister. Wally said that he could use your help with dinner." Heather looked at her then back at Randal. "Do you have anything to say?"

"Yes. I'm sorry, Laney. I know that I hurt your feelings, but that don't mean I want to move. I like the snow and my friends. And I can't catch the bus if you take me way far away."

She skipped out of the room and Laney sat down. She wanted to cry, to sob like a little baby herself, but she knew from past experience that tears were as useless as her stepmother had been. So when strong hands pulled her from the couch and into an equally sturdy chest, she went willingly and held onto Randal like a lifeline she'd never had before.

"She hates me." He said that she didn't, but a lot had happened to her. "Yes, well, me too. I've been uprooted. Brought here to six feet of snow in a hundred degrees below zero winter. I have no boots or a decent coat, and I have my family coming out here to make trouble for us. Oh, and I'm an immortal that has all kinds of magic that will be helpful, but for what, I have no idea."

"Yes, you have. And there are other things too that you didn't list. You have a family here, not just mine but a great many others, who will drop everything to come to your aid. And have, by the way, to make this better for your sister. Also, there is a lot to be said for a hundred below zero weather. It's very good snuggling weather. But, most importantly, did venting make you better? I mean, do you feel better now?" She looked up at him. "The reason I ask is, I think you need a nap. Kids get cranky when they need a nap."

"I'm not a child." He said nothing, but she felt like one in that moment. "I'm whining. I don't usually whine at all, but as you pointed out, it's been a hell of a week for us."

"I have some news that's not going to help you with your whiney behavior. Your parents will be here the day after Christmas. I know you have to return to your home, but I'd rather you dealt with them here, while there is family around. If you would rather leave and go out there and not have the support you need, then we'd go too. Just to keep you safe. They're not going to be thrilled about you taking Heather away from them." She asked him if he knew what they were planning. When he didn't answer, she looked up at him and asked again. "If you're asking me if they want Heather because they love her, then no, that's not the plan. Rosemarie thinks to take her back with them, get more support from the state, and then kill her. Not violently, she is thinking, but she doesn't want to raise her any more now than when she was born."

"I can't let them take her. They'll...Heather is all I have left in this world." He let her go when she pulled away, and she felt like a cold blanket had been laid over her. Shivering, she went to stand in front of the fireplace. "I don't have a leg to stand on, do I?"

"No. I'm sorry, but my sister-in-law found a will that names your stepmother as guardian of Heather. And I've had my brother Tanner—he's an attorney—looking into a few things, and he said that with your lifestyle, living alone in a gambling town, you'll not get her either. Your parents will be arrested but not right away, and that means that they'll not be able to take her anyway. Like I said, the Feds and Chloe want something that will stick so they spend time in prison. But I'm afraid that you will be turned down as well." She pointed out that she was her sister. "Yes, a sister that she's not seen very often. And even though I can understand the reasoning behind it, they'll wonder why you didn't offer support to her when she needed it."

"That isn't right." He nodded and sat when she did. "What do I have to do? Just leave here now? Without her?"

"I have a plan, but you're not going to like it." She nodded and asked him what it was. "Marry me. I know that you think this is a trick, but hear me out. My name means something. Not just here, but all over the state. My brothers are upstanding men, Trent is the pack leader, and four of them are married with families of their own. My grandparents as well as my parents are here for support, and Heather is a student of mine. I know her well, and I'm well thought of in our district, as I said."

Her first instinct was to tell him no, hell no, but she wasn't one to jump in with both feet and have herself drown. And right now, she was drowning. Her sister might not know her as well as she'd like, but letting her go with her mom was going to be the worst thing that ever happened to either of them. Getting up to pace, she thought of all the things that marrying this man would mean for them. Not just her and him, but for Heather as well.

"Tell me why again they're going to be put in jail." He told her things that she didn't know, as well as a couple that she was aware of. "And this Social Security scam, that's not enough to get them into trouble? It seems to me that that's a no brainer."

"Rosemarie could always say that she had no idea that Sally Anne had applied for her a card too, nor that she knew she was going to claim her." Laney said they'd have that kind of story if it came out. "Yes. And without Sally Anne around to naysay her plan, then she'd get off. Not entirely, but enough that she'd only be fined and not put in prison."

"What about my dad? Lance Price was never a man that was in trouble until he married Rosemarie Prichard. He was a good man; not a great father, but a good man." Randal didn't say anything. She knew that he had more bad news, and she wasn't sure she could take much more. "Would you like to go out to dinner? With me? I know that it's off the wall, but I really need to do something fun. Just for tonight."

"Sure. I'd love that. I have a few more gifts to pick up anyway. The day after tomorrow is Christmas. Do you need to do any shopping?" She did. Since it had only been her a few days ago, she'd not bought a single thing, not even a tree. "All right. There is something in the magic that I think you can benefit from. You can dress yourself. What I mean is, think of something you'd like to wear and it'll be there."

A plethora of things ran through her mind, and she had to stop and think of things that she could wear out. For some reason the thought of a sexy little nighty with barely any covering came to mind over and over. Laney was afraid that she knew why…this man was too sexy for his own good, and she wanted a piece of him. A huge hunk of him, as a matter of fact.

When she was dressed in warm clothing—boots, gloves, and a hat—she felt better. Warmer too. As they made their way out to his Jeep, she thought of what she'd be doing right now. Wally said that he'd enjoy having the little miss around. He had some projects for her to take care of with him. Plus the thought of not walking around in the snow to do shopping seemed sort of depressing. Laney was smiling when Randal started the car up and they took off. She might enjoy the snow too.

CHAPTER 3

Rosemarie hated the cold. If she could have, she would have gone back down to Florida and been done with it. She might still, once they had her kid back and she was free of her. Looking over at Lance, she asked him again if he was okay driving. He glared at her and told her that he'd not wrecked, so he was fine.

"I was only going to say I could drive a little bit too if you wanted me to." He told her that he was sorry, but he was a little on edge. "Yes, me too. I hate Ohio. I have no idea why Sally Anne thought it was a good place to flop at."

"She had to be far enough away so that no one would put together that you two were related and running that scam. I still don't like that part of it. I know that it helped us, but it's the government, and they can be harsh when you break their laws." She smiled when she thought of the amount of money they'd both made off that kid. "What are your plans for her when we get there? She doesn't know us any more than we do her. Maybe she'll not want to come with us. Have you thought of that?"

"I don't care. We need her to come along, and we'll make sure she has it right in her head too. I don't want anyone looking into shit about us." He asked her what she meant. "You know, the fact that we've been saying that she's right there with us all along. That'll make people think about our card and how much we been getting, 'cause they think we already got her now."

"Yeah, that'll be bad. What do we tell them if they ask why we don't? I'm sure you have that all worked out." She told him what she and Sally Anne had come up with. "That's a good one. She was visiting her sister. I like that. And if they ask about the income tax, what then?"

"That we didn't know that she was scamming the government, and that we honestly thought that since we was supporting her, we could take her out on our taxes and such. That way, without her being able to blame me, she'll be in trouble, not us." She hated that her little girl was gone. "I'm gonna miss her so much, Lance. She was such a good girl. Not at all like your daughter is."

"She's been a sore spot on us since we got together. I think sometimes that I didn't do right by her, leaving her the way I did. But Carol, she was a good woman and always teaching Laney things that would put her ahead in the world. Which I guess is a good thing. Like figuring her checkbook out for herself and all. I don't know why you never learned about a check and all. Unless it's because there was never any money. Is that it?" Rosemarie nodded. "When I met you, my love, it was the best thing that could have happened to me. I feel so free all the time."

"I do as well, Lance. You've been really good to me too." She watched the cars going around them and wondered why they were going so fast, like they were trying to get someplace that was giving away free shit. "These people are insane driving like this. You just be careful, honey, and we'll get there when we do. I hate that we're missing the funeral and all, but we'll be there in one piece."

Rosemarie had tried to call Laney to ask her for money to help them get home to bury her sister several times over the last few days. She'd not told Lance that she had her number. He'd be calling her all the time, just to make up to her about what he'd supposedly done to her. But of course Laney wasn't answering her phone. Rosemarie did wonder if someone had called her yet about Sally Anne's death, and hoped that they hadn't. Rosemarie would love to be the one that told her a month from now that her poor sister and her wonderful husband were dead. Rosemarie looked out the window and thought of the first time she'd met the girl.

"My lord, you're a fat one, aren't you?" Lance hadn't been as nice to her as he was now, and he told her to hush. "Well, look at her, Lance. She looks like a ten-pound sausage in a one-pound sack. You should move away from the table sooner, honey, if you want to get yourself a man."

"I don't need a man in my life." Rosemarie told her that since she was a little kid yet, she'd figure it out later. "I'm going to save my money and become something. Daddy is going to send me to college."

He hadn't, not after Rosemarie had gotten done with him. There just wasn't any money for the kid and college, not with them spending it like they had it. And in the beginning, they had had a lot. Besides, Sally Anne had expressed an interest in hair styling, and they'd had to put out the money for that. Then after that, there was always something that they needed or wanted more than paying for college. About a week before her eighteenth birthday, Laney had come to them about her mom's insurance.

"She said that I was the beneficiary. I want to use that money for my education." Her dad had laughed then and said it was all gone. "What do you mean, it's all gone? You can't touch that money. It belonged to me."

"Well, you had to eat, didn't you? You needed shoes and a good coat, didn't you? You think that kind of thing grows on trees?" Rosemarie watched her man and wondered why he'd never said a thing about any insurance, and was ready to pounce on his head when Laney just walked away. "There isn't no insurance that I can find. Carol talked about it, how she had set it up for Laney to have money for school, but I can't find anywhere where she actually took out the policy."

"Why didn't you just tell her that?" Lance said it was more fun to make her think they'd spent it all. "Yeah, well, it was fun seeing her face crushed like that. She's not a nice person, that daughter of yours."

"I don't know. I guess I never noticed it before you came into my life. She's nothing but a goody two shoes, as you said." He'd been sad about that. Rosemarie hadn't been sure then or now if it was because of her, or that his little girl was disappointed and upset with him.

It wasn't long after that when Laney moved out of the house and started working. She could be persuaded to send them money when they needed it for rent and such at first. Even to send some to her sister when she called. But then that had dried up as well. No cards, no money, and when they called, she rarely answered her phone. It was like she didn't want a thing to do with any of them anymore. Then Heather had been born.

Rosemarie would have thought she was too old to have another kid. But when Heather was born, all she could think about was taking it out and smothering it. All it did was squall and scream. Wanting its diaper changed, or something to eat. When Sally Anne called her one night and told her how she'd lost her own baby, they'd come up with a plan to use the kid for some extra cash. But Sally Anne kept it instead of selling it off for more money like she was supposed to.

Sally Anne pulled the same scams that the two of them had before Lance came along. Putting Sally Anne's name on the charity Christmas trees in the malls. Going to the food pantry with her all wrapped up in her arms got her more food than they could eat. Also, Rosemarie would stand on the corner with her daughter and people would drop off money in the hat she'd beg for it in. And all the while, she'd never had to pay rent or utilities, and she had herself and Sally Anne a nice home to stay in. That was, until her daughter turned eighteen and all that dried up like a hot day in the sun.

"You think that she was true to me about how much she was making on the scams? It's too bad that she had to die just before Christmas. We sure did rake it in this time of year." Lance said he had no idea, but he didn't have any reason not to believe her. "Yeah, she was a good girl, my Sally Anne. And to be cut down in the prime of her life like she was. I'm going to see about finding her dealer and suing them. There might be some money in that too. He probably sold her some bad shit and she paid the price, my little girl."

"I don't know if I'd say much about that, Rosemarie. They'd know that you knew about her and drugs, and that could be a bad thing since we're going to take Heather back with us. But you are right, the two of them made a nice couple, I think. I mean, they sure did look like a wedding cake topper when she sent us some of her pictures." She smiled at Lance, thinking that he never said that sort of nice things about his own daughter any more. "I'll tell you about something that I've been thinking about, Rosemarie. I'm a little worried about what Laney might say if someone called her. Laney might be a pain in the ass, but she isn't stupid about things. She might fight us for custody of Heather."

"Maybe that's a good thing. She might want to buy her off us. Of course, you'll have to tell her that she has to follow the rules we had with her sister." She was warming to the idea. "In fact, I think we should sort of charge her rent for her having the kid. You know, so we can be compensated for the loss of her. Oh, and the funeral costs too. We can tell her that we have to pay it, and have her pay us monthly for that too."

"I thought you said that the city paid for her and Clay's funeral. If she were to want the kid, then we'd not have to mess with it. It'll be a strain on us, having that kid around all the time. I mean, just having my daughter around when her mom died was hard on me. And I had my parents to help out." Rosemarie hadn't liked them either. They were as straight-laced as Lance used to be, and sometimes still was.

"I know, but we have each other and we'll work this out for us." Laney would take the kid from them, but at a price. "How much do you think we can get for her? I'm thinking about ten grand, and another five each month after that."

"That sounds like a goodly amount, don't you think? I mean, she has to live too. I mean, we are giving her our only child together, but we don't want to break her, do we?" He laughed a little and she loved it. "I'm gonna need a few drinks before I can go much further, honey. Why don't you pop open that bottle you put in the back and we can get warmed up?"

She had several cases of the shit in the back, all of them taken right from the truck at their local bar. The man had left his delivery truck unattended, what did he expect to happen? But the cases of liquor would only go so far before they'd have to do something else. She wished now that they'd gotten several more of them instead of just the three that they had.

"Next time it pulls in, we're going to be ready for him. I got us lined up with a cart for it. That way when we unload it, we'll be able to carry it off like nothing at all." He told her that was a good plan. "But we have to be back right before New Year's. That truck is going to be like gold and you know it."

"Yes, for the New Year deliveries, I think you mean. It'll be well stocked, as well as some of the better brands that I used to drink too." She nodded at him. She sometimes forgot that he had come from an educated background, while she'd not even finished high school.

"Yes, it will be. I never thought of that. You think we should get the kid something? I mean, so far as she knows, she lost her momma. And if we want her to like us enough to come with us, we're going to have to be nice." Lance said he had it. He'd gotten her one of Sally Anne's old dolls that she'd left behind. "Well, aren't you just the right man for the job."

"When Laney lost her mom, she latched herself onto a dolly and never wanted anything to do with anything else. Everywhere she went, the doll was with her. She just never seemed to come around to me again, but sat in her room talking to it like she was too sad to speak to me." She pointed out that she hadn't liked her either. "No, she didn't. And you opened my eyes to all her odd behaviors. I'm telling you,

Rosemarie, I never knew I could like coasting through life like I have been with you. When Carol was alive, I was so straight and on point, it never occurred to me to be anything but that. I like my life now. It's exciting and fun. We get to do things I never did before."

She could tell that he was just saying those things. He was upset all the time about things. Money and taking extra food from the pantry when they didn't need it. And then there was the income tax, as well as the free housing. He was looking for a job again too. And she knew she'd have to put a stop to that soon.

But still, Rosemarie loved that he'd said those things to her. It made her feel all warm inside. Nobody but this man could make her feel like she was worthy and loved. As she watched the snow coming down around them, she thought of their years together and how much fun they'd really had, even though he could be a poop head when he got all business like with her. It had been an adventure, she would say that. And she loved him more than she did anyone else she'd shacked up with.

"Maybe when she pays us for the kid, we should go on a trip or something. Go someplace where it's warmer than Florida. With pretty sandy beaches and Adirondacks that you like." She had to think what that was…he was so much smarter than her. "Those wooden ones aren't my favorite, but I know how much you like to sit in them."

That was another thing that he did for her. Lance never made her feel stupid when she didn't know something. He'd just say something a different way for her to understand. The man was a marvel.

"Yeah, I'd surely like that. Sand and sun is enjoyable at

home, but to be someplace different would be nice. I'll look for someplace when we get back home. I'd like to just fill up on those little drinks with the umbrellas in them. I don't even care if they water it down a little for me to enjoy it if it's got fruit or shit in it." They both laughed. "But we ain't driving. This shit is for the birds. We'll go first class. I bet we could even hire us our own plane to get there with the kind of money that Laney is going to pay us. And she will. Her heart is just too tender not to."

Rosemarie wasn't going to take shit from his daughter anymore either. She just decided that. Laney was going to play ball with them or she'd be in deep trouble. The kind of trouble that Rosemarie could rain down on the girl would be monumental too. She had connections that nobody, not even her Lance, knew about. It would be worth any cost too, just to have the bitch out of her hair. Rosemarie knew that Laney was directly responsible for her little girl's death, she just wasn't sure how yet, but she knew it. And Laney was going to pay.

~~~

Laney hadn't ever wrapped gifts before on this scale. She had gone just a little overboard, she knew that, but once she got started, she had so much fun, she didn't even think about the cost. Which, Randal had told her several times that they could well afford whatever she wanted. When the bill came in, she knew that she'd be regretting the spending, no matter what he said. But she'd never forget how much she had enjoyed it.

"I brought you some refreshments, my lady." Wally wouldn't stop calling her that, so she had to grit her teeth whenever he did. When he smiled, she asked him if she'd been doing this wrong. "I don't believe there is a wrong way

41

to wrap gifts. I was just thinking how much fun you were having. And so is Master Randal. He is currently updating his class work and whistling. Since I've been here, I don't think I've heard him do that. You have been good for him."

"Yes, he might not think so when we're married." He smiled bigger and she laughed. "I'm not going to give into him, nor do I plan on making it easy on him. He's only doing this to help me with my sister."

"If you say so, miss. The family will be here in an hour. If you wish, I can have this finished for you in no time so that you might be ready for the service." She looked around. There was so much more for her to do, and tomorrow was Christmas. "The faeries have been waiting for you to say you are finished so that they might help, so you know. They are as excited as you to have so much to do for the holidays. And with a child in the house, they are beyond ready for some fun."

"I love having them here. They do take some getting used to, but they're all so sweet and nice to me. Yes, tell them to come and finish up for me, please." Before she was finished speaking, the room was filled with the tiny people. And once they started moving, she sat very still and watched.

They were so fast and full of energy. But it wasn't just that. They were efficient too. It seemed as if every movement they made was with purpose and reason. And as they moved around the room, picking up the rolls of paper, using the tape dispensers, she leaned back. The scissors were left alone, she noticed, as they just ran their hands along the rolls of colorful wrap and flew away with it. In less than ten minutes, they not only had the rest of the gifts wrapped for her, but the room was tidy again. Laughing, she stood up and one of them landed on her hand.

"Thank you, my lady. We so enjoy helping you." Laney told her it was her pleasure to watch them work. "We will help you in any way we can. We would also like to help you dress for your wedding today. The pip has watched the movie with the pretty cinder girl."

She knew that a group of faeries and or brownies was called a pip. But it took her a moment to realize what she was talking about with the cinder girl. Laney asked her if she had enjoyed the movie. And when she said that she had but the little faeries were wrong in her opinion, Laney laughed. "Yes, I've never seen a plump faerie, nor a brownie. I think you move too quickly and burn a great deal of energy."

They entered the room she'd been sleeping in, and she felt her heart take a little jump when she looked around. "This room is so much bigger than my whole apartment back home. And much nicer."

"You have excellent taste, my lady." Just as she was to correct her on just calling her Laney, not that it would do much good, she spoke again. "My name is Bane, I have been around a great many summers. We have taken a vote, and it has been deemed that I be your faerie. It is my honor to serve you, my lady."

"Wait. I don't understand. What do you mean, serve me? I'm not...just tell me what that means and we'll go from there." Bane grinned at her, and Laney had a feeling that she wasn't going to like this answer. "You're saying something with that smile that makes me nervous."

"I belong to you and only you. The only other persons who can make me do something that I do not wish to do are your mate, Randal, which he would never do, and the lady of the earth, my queen." Laney sat down and tried to think what it meant to own a person. Small yes, but she was a person. "You do not have to pay me, but to give me flowers when you wish. And I can do all manner of things for you. You will be surprised how much I can do for someone such as you. And it will never be a hardship to serve you, no matter what it is. We are so happy to have you here, making Master Randal so happy. And with you bringing the child into the home, we have so much to do and enjoy Lady Heather as well."

"You mean a human when you say someone like me?" Bane nodded. "Okay, but just to be clear, I'm not thrilled about the word owning. You can work for me, but I don't own you. All right?"

"Yes, my lady. Lord Randal told me that you would not like that word as well. When I asked him, he said that I should go easy with you, that you are new to us." Boy, Laney thought, that was an understatement. "He also told me that should you seem hesitant, that I was to tell you that he has a faerie as well. Also, I don't know if you've been told, but Wally, your cook, is a witch. He can do great things."

"Yes, that I knew." She looked around the room and wondered what she was doing here. Yes, she had agreed to marry Randal, and they had an understanding that it was in name only, but the man was driving her crazy.

When she'd come to him with her answer, he had been so sweet about it that she did want to give him a kiss. But he told her that he'd wait until she was ready. Whatever the hell that meant. She was ready all the time when he was around her. Even when he wasn't, she felt all hot and bothered just thinking about him.

"Mistress?" She looked at Bane and wondered again what

she was doing. "Are you unwell?"

"I don't know what I am. I'm confused. Overwhelmed. Overheated. I think that I'm also well over my head in this relationship with Randal. He's so sweet, but I have a feeling that it's only a façade or something." Bane just stared at her, as if she didn't know what to tell her. "I was wondering something. His mom, Christine. Is she…is she someone that I could talk to? I mean, is she as nice as she seems?"

"Oh yes. They all are. You should have them come here and talk to them." When she disappeared, Laney went into the bathroom to shower. The shower alone was as big as her closet, and the big closet was as big as her living room. Turning on the water, she stripped down and thought about marrying this man. Looking in the mirror, she thought about ever loving him.

"You are nuts, did you know that?" Her reflection had no comment. "You should not only have your head examined, but you should be committed too. Marrying a complete stranger just so you can keep your sister safe is nuts. And the fact that he is making you feel like a hotheaded teenager on your first date isn't the way to go into a name only relationship either. Yep, you're nuts."

The shower was a wonderful place to think. The water was nice and warm, and the jets hit her in all the right places and made her muscles relax. Laney had a feeling that the house, again, was taking care of her, but at the moment, she decided that she wasn't going to think about what it might be doing. When she finished, she stood in the stall and dried her hair. Doing one thing at a time and not thinking about everything was less devastating to her thought process.

Wrapping the towel around her body, she entered the

bedroom only to stop in her tracks. Six women, all of them family, were sitting around the room with tea and scones, another thing that she'd come to love here. Clearing her throat, they all turned to look at her.

"What would you have done had I come out of there naked?" Jas, Randal's grandmother, laughed and told her that they all had the same girly parts. "Yes, I suppose we do. However, my girly parts are not usually on display. Are yours?"

"Not unless it's a full moon. Bane said that you wished to speak to us." She had? Well, they were here now, and she might as well ask the hundred and one questions that were circling around in her head. "You are worried, I'm thinking. About what we might think about all this. Well, I for one am thrilled. You are a perfect fit in this family."

"You have no idea if I am or not." Laney tried the trick, the one that dressed her, and when she felt clothing cover her, she put the towel in the bathroom. "I might be a serial killer that kills men for their money after I marry them."

"You've never been married. You date very little. And usually with a man by the name of Dave Collar. He is your go to man when you need someone on your arm. His lover, and husband now, is Jamie Groves. They've been together for several years, and you love them both." Laney sat down as Joe continued. "You have forty thousand dollars and some change in your savings account right now. And you have a nice 401k that you can transfer to another fund whenever you like. A car that is older than you, and mostly sits in the garage because you don't like the traffic that comes with going around town; not to mention, you've come to love taking the city busing system. It gets you to and from work or wherever.

You are very cautious about investing, but you figure you have time so you invest wisely and carefully. I could do that for you. I have a knack."

"You have a knack for a lot of things, I guess." Joe nodded. "Why are you looking into my personal business?"

"Your parents are coming here. I want no surprises when they do." Laney said that she could have told her all this. "Yes, but I like to have a look too. You'd be surprised how much is out there that you might not know about. Most people think that they know everything there is to know about themselves, when they're just as much in the dark as most about their spouse or whoever. Like you, for instance."

"I see. And you know a great deal about me that you think I don't. Such as?" She told her what she knew. "Yes, that would be my stepmother's doing. And once I get the bill for whatever she's bought with a credit card that she's taken out in my name, I will take her to court. How many credit cards does she have in my name now?"

"None. I took care of that as well. She and your father have been using one to get here on your dime, and that will no longer get them gas nor a hotel should they stop. The fact that you might have been aware of her deeds makes me think that you also know that she applied for a house loan recently as well. That, of course, was canceled as soon as I found it. The bank, as you can well imagine, was most pleased that you warned them that you were not only not cosigning on her loan, but that you have nothing to do with anything else she has applied for." Laney thanked her. "It is my pleasure."

"They're in Ohio. They arrived in the state about an hour ago. They have been detained a couple of times, but nothing major. We want them to come here." Laney asked Chloe why.

She knew what Randal had said, but was worried that there was more to it now. "Because, my dear sister, we work better when we have all the cards. And the house will rule in this."

"Funny, using a card quote in this. But, you do know a great deal about me that has nothing to do with them. Why?" Jas smiled at her and told her because they wanted to make sure that she had help when it was needed. "I don't ask for help well."

"Yes, we've noticed that as well. Now, we'd like to give you a little knowledge about us. While Jas and Christine are wolves, that isn't all they are. They're immortal, the same as the rest of us, and that includes you and any children that you will have, as well as anyone that you and Randal call your own." She asked if that meant Heather. "It does. She will heal much faster than a normal human will. You would be surprised to know how handy that comes in when dealing with pricks."

Of all the women in the room, she thought perhaps she liked Marty the best. She was personable, as well as seemed like her…a normal person just trying to get by in this world. When they started telling her about the rest of the family and what they contributed to the clan, Laney listened with half an ear. She was getting married today, and she was terrified out of her mind. When someone snapped their fingers in her face, she looked at Jas, the grandmother to them all.

"I'm sorry. I didn't mean to be so rude." Jas told her she wasn't as she sat back down in her chair. "I don't want to be rude again, but why are you guys here? I mean, not just here in the house, but here with me. I'm sure that you have better things to do than to hang out with me."

"You're going to be our family in a few hours." She knew

that they were aware of why she and Randal were marrying, and it had little to do with the fact that they believed her to be his mate. "Randal is a good boy. And we just wanted you to feel welcome."

"But what if I leave here with Heather after my parents are dealt with? Don't you think it's a waste of your time to get to know me?" Jas just laughed. "I'm serious. It's going to be hard enough to leave as it is without taking you guys more into my heart. And Heather is going to be very upset."

"Why is it that you want to go? I'm not referring to the things you have out there. All of that, whatever it is, can be boxed up and brought here should you want. But what do you have there that holds you?" She said she had a job. "Yes, all right. Is it one you enjoy? Are there friends there that make it worth your while to go to work daily?"

"I love my job. And I'm very good at it. But no, I don't have all that many friends. I'm somewhat of a loner. I think it has to do with not wanting to spend money on things that are just silly. I don't drink because my dad does. Drugs are out of the question because of my sister, and I don't sleep around either." She said she knew that. "How do you know that? Is this another query about me someone looked up?"

"No. I can smell, as can the rest of us, that you're a virgin." That shut her up. She smelled like a virgin? "Don't be offended, my dear. We can also smell when you're ovulating, having a baby, and when you're sick or bleeding. It's the way of our beasts."

"This is very strange…you know that, don't you?" Jas told her that it was normal for them. "Yes, well, I'm not sure how used to that I can get."

"Oh, you will. And would you like to know something

else? My grandson is in love with you." She wanted to shake her head no, but she felt her heart twist up. Not in a bad way, but with excitement. "I see that you might be just a little in love with him as well. Aren't you?"

CHAPTER 4

Randal felt good. Not that he wasn't a little stressed, but he felt really good about this. Marrying Laney was going to give him everything in the world that he wanted, even if he had to wait for a while to get it. As he waited in the side room for the quick ceremony to begin, his dad came up to him and observed his tie. His own looked like Heather had tied it, and Randal wasn't sure but thought she could do a better job at it.

"How do you do that so well?"

He told him lots of practice as he worked on his dad's tie. "I wear one every day to school and during meetings. You almost have it right."

It took him less than a minute to get his dad fixed, but he knew that there was more to it than just the tie. Randal hugged him, as he did every day of his life, and told him how much he loved and respected him.

"Thank you, son. That means a great deal to me. I wanted to talk to you anyway." He handed him a small box, and he opened it. "That was your mom's when we first got engaged. I sort of messed up when I gave it to her. I got the horse before the cart, you might say. That's the wedding ring instead of the engagement ring I meant to give her."

"It's beautiful." He didn't bother telling his dad that he'd already purchased a ring for Laney. This would mean so much more to her, he thought. "Dad, I'm nervous. What if she wants to go out west again? I don't want to leave you guys."

"I know that, I do, and I worry about it too. But you have to follow your heart, and in this case, I'm thinking that she has it." He nodded and smiled at him. "You're a good boy, Randal. A teacher that everybody loves. Sometimes a little too much with them moms, but you handle that well too."

"I'm going to have to figure out a way to wear a ring so that everyone can see that I'm off limits more than ever." His dad laughed and told him that wouldn't matter to some. "But it does to me, and I want Laney to never think I'm encouraging them."

"She won't. I bet she might help you out with that too." Randal hugged his dad again. "I'm right proud to be giving her away. When she asked me and not my dad, I had to crow a bit. He is usually the one that gets those kinds of honors."

"Laney loves you, all of you, but she thinks you're the sweetest man she has ever met." His dad flushed a bright red. "Dad, I want her to be safe in all this. And for Heather to have a good home. Whatever happens with this, her going or staying, I'm going to make sure of that."

"Of that, I have no doubt." Randal nodded and looked at the others in the room with him when his dad spoke again. "You sure do have some fine brothers. I could not have asked for better sons had I put in an order for them and gotten them that way. You boys, you're men I guess now, but you'll always be my boys."

Giving his dad another hug, he sat down by the window and watched the snow coming down. Yesterday it had been about fifty and most of the stuff had melted off. Today it was just a light dusting, but they were expecting about ten inches overnight. He was excited to have his first Christmas as a husband with a family. And to bring them to his grandparents' house for the day was just icing on the cake. Things were looking up for him, he thought.

I thought you'd like to know that I've been watching the Price couple. I have to tell you, Randal, they're as odd as it comes. He asked Noah why he'd say that. *They are currently sitting alongside of the road having relations. Not sex...I'd never call this sex, but it's nasty.*

Randal burst out laughing and everyone in the room turned to stare at him. When he told them he was speaking to Noah, they went back to what they were doing. Randal asked him how far away they were.

I've given them some cash for some gasoline. I do want them to get there, but I don't care to feed their habit. The two of them are very drunk. How did someone as sweet as your future wife come from such a couple? Randal told him that only the father was hers. *Well, it makes no more sense than it did before. These people are nasty.*

Yes, well, they're going to be in for a rude awakening when they arrive. Anastasia is here with her men, waiting on them to make a move. Then there are three other agencies that also have warrants for their arrest. Noah told him that they'd only be stretched so far. *Perhaps, but they'll be put away for a good long time with the crap they all have on them.*

The sister, Sally Anne. You should know that she is the one that purchased the heroin that killed them both. That would mean murder, if anyone but you and I knew. I've found their dealer, a very unimpressive young woman that is no longer in business. Randal asked him what he'd done. *Nothing but give her the option of going to prison or stopping her dealings. Sadly, I don't think she'll hold to her promise.*

Thank you. Every day, it gets harder and harder to keep even kids in my class away from drugs. I hate to have anyone die over this, but there is sometimes only one way to deal with dealers. His dad told him it was time and Randal stood up. *I take it you're not going to make it to my wedding.*

I'm here. I just saw your bride. My goodness, what a lovely little thing she is. He thanked him. *If you would be so kind as to let her know that I need a small taste of her, I'll feel better. There are all kinds of terrible people in the world, and two of them are on their way to you now.*

They were all gathered in the judge's chambers, but you'd never think that with all the flowers and people in the room. Judge Williams, a good friend of the family, said that he'd never had such a beautiful bride nor setting to make this right. He stood right in front of the tree that was decorated in the gaudiest decorations that he'd ever seen. But somehow, it was perfect.

There were not just round balls for ornaments, but also small plastic guns and grenades. There were also things like warrants with no name on them, petitions too. Tiny police hats and badges. He had seen it from a distance at first, but knew that seeing it up close hadn't made any improvements on it. It was the sort of oddity that made his day.

Slipping the ring on Laney's finger, he looked at her face as he repeated the words back to her. He was to love, honor, and hold her forever. But when he was finished, he added his own words, ones from his heart.

"I also promise to keep you safe, hold you when you need it, and let you have the lead when you're braver and stronger than I am. Which, I have to tell you, according to my family, might be a lot more than you think." They all laughed. "I will love you for the rest of my days, honor you in ways that no one will ever question, and I will keep you in my heart."

She looked at him then, and he could see her love for him. It surprised him, mostly because she'd never said the words to him, but he felt it all the way to his heart as it wrapped around him. Randal nodded to the judge and he said her part, which she repeated back to him. Randal started to kiss her when he said it was time.

"Hold on, buddy. It's my turn." Again his family laughed, but he held her hands and waited. "I've not been brave in all my years. Stupid at times, yes, but never brave. I'm hoping that with you at my side, I can start to enjoy life. Be loved by someone that doesn't have to, but wants to. To have someone like you enjoy my company and laugh when you think I'm funny. I have never said these words to anyone before, and I'm so glad that I can say them to you now. Randal Calhoun, I love you with all that I am, all that I will ever be, and I love that you have not forced anything onto me that would hurt me. Thank you."

He kissed her then, and then again when it wasn't nearly as satisfying as he wanted. Holding her to him, loving her, they were pronounced man and wife just as one of his brothers popped the cork to one of the bottles of champagne that had been brought in for the occasion.

Randal let her be hugged by his family. His brothers made a big show of welcoming her to the family, and warned her that she was in for a big letdown with him as her husband. Lucky for him, he supposed, she gave as good as she got, and protected his manliness with just as many jabs back at them. He had fallen in love with her all over again.

Holding Heather's hand when she took his, he knew that this was making her just as happy as it was him. She had stability, something that she'd probably never experienced before in her young life. And she had people that loved her.

They were going to have a small reception at his parents' house, but he had plans right now. Searching for the room that Tanner had told him had a lock on the door, just in case he needed it, he took his lovely new bride down the hall in long hungry strides. As soon as he found it and shoved her inside, she was all over him as much as he was her.

"Hurry." He said he didn't want to muss her up. "Muss away. I'm so needy right now I could almost come with just you touching me. Christ, who knew that a wedding could do this to a person?"

He tore her dress from her shoulders. The shiver that she gave him, the show of her need, had his wolf stretching under his skin. When she opened his shirt without unbuttoning a single button, his beast took him.

"Randal? What the fuck is going on?" He'd not exchanged so much as a little blood with her, so he couldn't let her know it was all right. Pawing at her panties, she seemed to understand and took them off. "If he does more than just want me naked, I'm going to kill you both."

His wolf wanted his mate too. So when she was naked before them, his wolf lunged at her and licked her pussy. She came almost immediately and spread her legs wider for him. That was all he needed as an okay to take more of her into him, and his wolf wasn't going to pass up an opportunity to show his mate how much he loved her as well.

"Stop. No more." He took his body back and stood up. "Christ, I had no idea. Someone should have.... No, that would have been a little more awkward than having any other conversation with your grandma."

"Tell me again." She looked at him with a beautiful smile. "Tell me that you love us. Tell me how much I mean to you."

"You make me come like that a lot and I'll say whatever you want." He kissed her on the mouth, then put his forehead to hers. "I love you, Randal. So very much. I cannot believe I thought that I'd never fall in love with anyone, and you come along and make me not just love you, but need you as well."

"As much as I'd like to take you right here against the door, I want to take you home and make love to you in our bed. Several times." She nodded and told him that she was all right with that. "Then when you've rested a little bit, I'm going to start all over. And over and over."

"I'm sorry." He asked her what she was sorry about. "I'm not sure really, but I am. I think because when you took me on, you took on my family. And I came with extra baggage. My sister."

"I love your sister. She's a good girl, and I love having her around. And someday, when we're not being rushed into things, I want to adopt her. Make her my little girl." She told him again that she loved him. "And I you, my heart. Forever and a day, you will be my one and only true love."

The limo was there for them when they left the courthouse. He was glad at that moment that they had the ability to manufacture clothing with just a thought. Otherwise they'd be having to explain why they were both naked, or nearly so.

He pulled her onto his lap when the doors were closed and kissed her. There wasn't time for him to make her his yet, but that didn't stop him from giving her all that he could. Randal thought she came about a dozen more times before they pulled up in front of his grandparents' house, and was glad to see that she was slightly wobbly, because he was painfully full himself.

As soon as they entered the house he knew that something had happened. But what it was he'd have to wait to find out. The celebration had to come first, and he was glad that his family had thought enough of them to hold off ruining things for her. But that didn't stop him from asking Chloe about it.

Her parents have robbed a liquor store. Well, not so much her parents as her stepmother. I've been thinking about this, and I think that her dad is sort of in the dark about a lot of things going on there. I don't know why, because he's not as innocent as most, but he might not have a clue about a lot of it. She wasn't caught, but we know it was her. I think she's pulled this same scam before. While the truck is being unloaded, they take what they want and then run off. The only reason they gave themselves away this time is that one of them dropped one of the cases they were taking. Like I said, I don't know that he was involved, but she was for sure. And I think she is the one that plans and talks him into whatever scam she has cooking. He asked if anyone was hurt. *No. No one was around, so that was all they did. I think, as I said, they've done this before, and I have someone looking into it in their home state. Randal, these people are much worse than we first thought if they're both in on this. There is evidence that they might have been in on a bank robbery, as well as the black market for babies.*

Christ. Chloe agreed with him. *These babies, do I want to know where they got them? Or is that still something that you're*

58

looking into?

The local hospital and clinic where they live. Also, there is a baby clinic that she, mainly, goes to as well. Sixteen children all under the age of four have been kidnapped. He took the plate of food that Laney handed him, and he could tell that she knew something was up. But instead of asking him, she kissed him and told him later. *She's going to be hurt by this. It looks like her sister was supposed to sell Heather too, but for some reason didn't.*

I'll tell her later. He would too, all of it, holding her while he was at it. But there was cake and fun going on now, even if it was a little somber. Randal wanted them to just leave them alone, but he knew that as soon as this was done, he was taking his new family on a long trip. Someplace that no one would know who they were.

~~~

Laney wasn't sure what to do with herself. Her hands were sort of shaky and her knees felt like they were knocking together. But she could do this, she told herself. And the sooner she left the bathroom, the sooner she could be with her husband.

Husband. She had one now. And a good one at that. Looking in the mirror, talking to herself again, she told herself that she was lucky that he knew all about her family before he married her, or he might have run.

"No, I wouldn't have." She looked at him, not even hearing the door open she'd been so nervous. "I wasn't sure what you were doing in here. I could hear you talking and wondered if you had company. Do you usually talk to yourself?"

"Yes. But only in the mirror. I know that sounds off my noodle, but I usually give myself pep talks when I'm about to do something that I've never done before." He nodded but didn't make fun of her. "Do you have any strange habits that I need to know about before I catch you at them?"

"Let me see." He grinned. "I take my lunch to school. Everyday. And while that sounds like something normal, I should tell you that I eat sardines and crackers. Sometimes with cheese, sometimes not. And then for dessert, I have a dozen Swedish fish. I'm addicted to them, but only allow myself a dozen of them."

"Why a dozen? I mean, is that the one serving count on them or something?" He told her he thought it was five. "So you like to be a rebel?"

"No. I would eat an entire box of them at one sitting, but this way, it's my treat." She laughed when he did. "Also, there are things you should know too. I hate hot cocoa. Not just the taste, but the smell as well. And cinnamon. It gives me a headache."

She sat on the counter when he came in the room with her. He sat on the vanity chair and took her foot into his hands. As he massaged it, working soreness out of it that she'd not known she had until then, Laney thought of the things she didn't care for.

"I don't care for foo-foo. I mean, I don't mind some pictures on the wall, a throw over the back of the couch, but no vases of dried flowers. Unless they mean something. I don't buy unless it's on sale, marked down several times, and then I will even ask for more of a discount. And I do not buy things that I don't need, either." He told her that his sisters were like that. "I know. They told me that they came from nothing. Except for Joe, but she still doesn't purchase something without a lot of thought. Why are you doing this?"

"To relax you. You're tense and we can feel it." She asked

him who. "My wolf and me. As most shifters, we refer to ourselves as two separate beings. I'm not sure why, but that's what we do. My wolf has thoughts and ideas. Some of them are about you, but mostly it's how to keep us all safe."

"Would it be all right if I asked you some questions?" He nodded and took her other foot into his hands. "What about children? Did you want them? And will they be wolves?"

"I want as many as you want to have. It's your body, and I'd never presume to tell you what to do with it." She felt her foot crack and thought of how good it felt as he continued. "They could be wolves or some part of them. Since you're not a wolf, not even a made one, they could be part to whole wolves. But they'll be immortal, the same as us. And marked. By the demon, Richard."

"Yes, Jas told me about him. I can't believe the trouble your family has had." He smiled at her and sat back on the chair. "Now, my family is coming here, and you know something about that too. Will you not keep things from me? I know that we were at our wedding and then the party afterwards today, but please don't keep things from me."

"I have no plans to. But as you pointed out, today was special, and I wanted it to be that way for you as much as I could." She nodded. "Your stepmother robbed a liquor truck this morning. Not caught, but there is a record of her doing it. Chloe isn't sure if your dad was involved, but to her, it doesn't look like it. Not this time anyway. Also, they've stolen children, mostly babies, and sold them for cash."

He told her everything that he knew, and she wasn't sure she wanted to believe him. She did, but this was beyond what she thought they were up to. And the fact that Heather would have been sold too made her heart ache more. She asked him if there was any way to get the children back.

"Joe and Chloe are looking into it, but I'd not hold out much hope. Unless they have something that belonged to the children, there isn't any way for us to track them down. Joe can find them, but only if there is something of the children's that she can touch that hasn't been washed. I'm sorry." She nodded, hurt about what those parents were going through because of her parents. "I love you, Laney."

"I love you too. But they're terrible, aren't they? I mean, even beyond what I thought they were up to, and that's bad enough, but they're tearing apart families too." He nodded. "And it could have been my sister too. Who knows if there were other children that...? Christ, it boggles the mind to think of who else might be out there that's related to me. My dad wasn't like this before her. I'm not blaming this all on Rosemarie, but he wasn't a monster like this before."

"Perhaps he was, but your mom kept him in line. Or as Chloe and Joe think, he isn't as involved as she is. He might not know the entirety of what she's done or doing." She started to cry and he stood up and held her. "I'm sorry to bring this up now. But I told you that I'd let you know when we got back here."

"I'm glad that you did. Otherwise I might not have been fun." He lifted her chin up so that he could kiss her and she held onto him. "I bet that you're not in the mood now, are you?"

He rocked into her. His cock was thick and hard, and she wanted to touch him. When he rocked into her again, she took her thick robe off and dropped it to the floor. The look in his eyes made the chill she had now seem well worth it.

"I want you right now, against this counter. The wall or

the floor. I'd take you in the shower." She giggled and he smiled. "Yes, that did sound like a children's book. But the things I want to do with you and to you are not childish at all."

"Take me, Randal." He lifted her up, his body firmly pressed against hers. When he took her to the bedroom and stood her next to the bed, he kissed her with hunger that matched her own.

He laid her out on the bed and stood over her. She thought that she'd be uncomfortable laying there with him staring at her so hard, but she felt pretty, sexy even. And when he started unbuttoning his shirt, she watched his every move, her mouth watering as much as her pussy did.

"Can you hurry?" He told her that he could, but he was enjoying this too much. "I'm very needy right now. I mean, I suppose I could do it by myself."

"You could, but I'm thinking what I have in mind for you will be so much better." He got down on his knees when he had his shirt off. "I'm going to eat you now. Then when I'm through with that, I'm going to taste all of your body once more, and mark you with my teeth."

She shivered again. Christ, he was going to kill her if just his words could do this to her. As he made short work of her nighty, careful not to tear it too much, she was finally naked. And he still was being so gentle with her.

"I'm hurting." She asked him if she could help him. "Oh, you will. But I want you to know that, because I'm barely hanging on here. I need you with a passion that I've never had before."

"I can live with that." He said that he might hurt her. "I'm okay with that as well. I need you. Very much. Can we get on with it?"

His laughter seemed to break something tense inside of him. He stood up then, pulled his pants off, and fisted his cock. She had a brief moment of fear...he was so fucking huge. When he laid down beside her, she wrapped her hand around him and he moaned. She sat up and then crawled on top of him. She felt his cock stretch even larger.

"Sit on me." She had to figure out how to do that. She'd read about it, of course, riding a man, but since she'd never done it, it was strange. Sliding down over him, she was careful to go slowly, not just to make him suffer as he had her, but to enjoy watching his face. And when she came down hard, with his help, nothing could have prepared her for the most intense pain she'd ever felt.

Randal was talking to her. What he was saying wasn't as important as what he was making her feel. The pain was subsiding now, so she listened to him. She looked down at him when he told her that he'd never do that again.

"Never? That's a very long time to go without sex, don't you think?" He grinned, charming and cute like she knew he used on his parents and grandparents. "I don't know...will I have to find me someone else to —?"

She was suddenly on her back and he was deeper inside of her, his hands over her body, his mouth following the same path. Never in all her life did she think that anyone had been this thorough with her. Not even as an infant and being bathed by her mom.

He made love to her, his hands and mouth soothing any discomfort that she had. And when he took her, his body sliding in and out of hers, Laney came hard enough that the world blinked out for a moment. Then she centered and she knew, right then, that it would always be like this with him. Intense and full of love.

No part of her was untouched, unloved by him. Every place that he nipped at her skin, it wasn't painful but an awakening of her body. Each time he kissed the small hurt, she felt like she'd been given new life, her body came alive. And she knew that he'd do this to her, make her feel like this, every time that he touched her.

"Come for me, love." Her body was at his command. And when she screamed out her release, simply because she couldn't contain it any longer, he held her, his body taking hers even higher than he had before. And at his "again," her mind soared with her body, up to the stars and back again.

Then the world simply winked out. She was sure she had died...every cell in her body exploded and renewed. As she settled in the bed, her body spent, her mind gone, love surrounded her in a cocoon and Laney was safe. And loved. Laney was loved like she'd never been before.

"I love you, Randal." He said that he loved her as well, pulling her body to his. She snuggled to his heart. This was what she'd missed her entire life, someone to love her without any conditions or rules.

CHAPTER 5

TJ was both glad and depressed that the holiday was over. Christmas had been the best that any of them had ever had. The children, TJ knew, made it the way it was. And soon, not too many months from now, there would be more children, more babies to bounce on his knees. As he waited for his tea to cool enough to sip it, he thought of all the gifts that had come his way, and thought that perhaps his favorite one, though he'd not say so, was the one from all of them, and signed with love that he felt every single day.

The picture of all his sons together had been a surprise. What surprised him even more was that they weren't all dressed in their finery, but in regular clothing, things that they wore every day. Trent had worn a polo shirt, Tanner a suit and tie. Even Randal had on a tie, but without a jacket. A polo for Scott, and Elijah wore a tee shirt. Sterl had on a paint stained apron, with a bit of paint on his face. It was perfect in that it wasn't perfect.

"I was thinking that you and I need to take a long vacation." He looked at his dad and asked him why he'd want to go with him. "Because you're my son. And I'd like to spend some quality time with you."

"I don't know if you realize this or not, but I have grandchildren coming soon. I'd like to be here for them." His dad sat down in the chair across from him and glared, telling him they were his grandchildren as well. "Then you can understand why I'd not want to take a trip right now."

"But you're not ruling it out." He shook his head. For as much as he fussed at his dad, he did love him very much. "I was thinking you and me, we'd drive down to the mountains and see us a show at one of them places in Tennessee. The Grand Ole Opera. Whatcha think?"

"I think you're nuts, but that does sound good." Another glare and TJ laughed. "Why? I mean, really, why do you want to spend time, more time than we do here, together with me? Is it something that I need to know, and you're softening the blow by taking me on a trip? Oh, I get it, you're taking me there to lose me. Won't work... I know my own address."

"Why are you being so dadburned mean for?" TJ said he was in a good mood and was kidding him. "Well, I was too until you started spouting off about leaving you there. I was thinking that we'd take the boys too. Make a manly time of it."

"I don't know, Dad. Seriously, they're all so busy right now. Pack and new mates. Babies coming along. To be honest, you saying that you wanted to spend time with me alone felt sort of good." His dad leaned back in his chair. "What's going on?"

"Your mom, she's upset with me." He asked him what he'd done to her now. "Why do you think I did a dadburned thing wrong?"

"Because Mom only gets upset when you do something. What is it? And how much is it going to cost you to get her on your good side again?" Dad got up to pace, but he didn't speak. TJ sipped his tea and watched him. He'd get around to it sooner or later.

"You remember a few weeks back, when I said I was going to open myself an auction place? I know you thought I was joshing you, but I wasn't. Anyway, I made me some inquiries about it, and there ain't really much in the need for one, so you know. And I'd not be all that good at it anyway. I like to be sociable, and that's not going to make me any money or sell much. But then I got to thinking about them grandbabies that are coming, and how we'd be taking them places, and that our car just ain't big enough to haul them around in." His dad could never tell a straight-line story when one that was as curvy as a beautiful woman would do better. "I got me one."

"Got you one what? A building? An auctioneer license? A new car?" Dad glared harder. "Dad, you mentioned like six things, and then say you got one. What did you get?"

"A motor home." Dad sat down. "I was thinking about them kids, I swear it. But I thought that we, your mom and I, could take a trip too in it. Your mom, she likes to travel and all. And taking them kids places, it'll be easier on us if we're not stopping every ten minutes to go to the bathroom and such. Plus, they can nap and all. I was thinking of all the fun we'd have."

"And you're wondering why Mom is mad at you." He nodded. "Did you think that maybe she might have wanted to go with you to pick this out?"

"She don't know nothing about cars and such. And she wasn't with me when I got the idea. I got us a good deal on it too." TJ just waited for his dad to get the point. "I guess she would be spending time in it, but it's not like I didn't have her in mind. She might not have liked the color or something, is that what you're waiting on me to get?"

"Yes, something like that. Mom will be spending time in it with you, and she does spend a great deal more time with the kids than you do too. Changing their diapers or whatever needs to be done. She might have thought that the one you got wasn't big enough, or didn't have enough beds in it. Her input might be the difference between you having to take a car too to travel with them, and having plenty of space for you all. Additionally, she might have wanted to have a little say so about the kitchen area."

"I never thought that far ahead, I guess. And she was saying something about the room in it. It's not giant, like I should have gotten us." TJ said that not too big might be better. "Yeah, I think you might be right on that. I know that I can take it back. I think I will. Right now. Yes, sir, I'm going to do that and take your mom along with me."

After his dad left, talking like he'd been the one that had thought it all the way through, TJ sipped his tea again. It was just now cool enough to drink. When Tanner came into the room with him, he hid his smile behind his cup. This was going to be a doozy, he knew it.

"I'm a single man." TJ told him that he was aware of that. "And you know as well as I do that she's coming here. Probably already here as far as things are going for me."

"Who?" His low growl had TJ laughing. "Son, I don't know if you're aware of this, but your Grandda just left me. He's as clear as a stone bell about things too. So if you got something on your mind, I'm afraid that I'm going to need a bit more information."

"My mate." TJ nodded, still fighting the fact that he was nearly blue with laughing. "She's lurking out there around the corner, and any minute she's going to come here and make demands on me. I know it."

"Lurking? I don't know about that, Tanner. The women in this family don't lurk. Unless they're sneaking up on the bad guys. Then there might be some lurking. And what are you all tied up about? You afraid of your mate?" Tanner said he wasn't afraid of anyone. "Oh, then it's the thought of being happy that's got you all twisted up in knots."

"I'm not going to be happy." TJ just cocked a brow at his tone. "I'm sorry, but I don't want a mate. I don't have time to be all spongey and gooey like the rest of them are."

"Spongey and gooey? Tanner, what makes you...? Never mind. All right then. I'll help you out with that when the time comes. If I find her lurking about, do you want me to bash her in the head or just turn her in the wrong direction?" He asked him to be serious. "I am. I got me a bat around here somewhere. Or I can just be my wolf and tear into her."

"I don't want her dead." TJ nodded and said nothing. "You're not being serious about this, are you? I don't want you to kill anyone."

"I don't want to either, but I also don't want you upset. It hurts me in ways I can't explain to see my kids upset." Tanner got up to pace, something TJ was sure that they'd learned from their grandda, just as he had. "Why are you not wanting to be found by your mate? And if I was you, I'd not mention anything to the rest of them about being gooey or lurking. They might take offense."

"Have you seen the way Trent acts when Joe is around?

Like a simpleton." TJ, wisely, said nothing as he sipped more tea. "Then the other day, I asked Sterl to go to the movies with me, and you know what he said? He had to ask Marty if it was all right. She might have plans."

"So you didn't go?" He said that they had, but he was missing the point. "No, I don't think I am. You are, but not me on this one. You think your mom would be happy with me if I just took off on some night of fun with you when she had something planned for us? A nice dinner or a movie or something? She'd have both our heads."

"That's not the same thing." He asked him why not. "Because they're my brothers, not my parents."

"Tanner, that makes no sense whatsoever. I don't know what's got you so all fired up, but that there, that made me think you're just grasping at straws. What is it really?" Tanner sat down, his face full of glum, like he'd been picked last for the big game. "Tell me and I'll help you work it out."

"Dad, I have my life just the way I want it. A mate is going to come in, change things around, and want more of my time. I don't have time for anything anymore. Not even dating." TJ nodded, pushing his empty cup away while his son lambasted having a mate. "She's going to be this macho woman that can shoot better than me, even do my job better than me, and I'm going to look like a sap."

"Yes, you are." Tanner looked shocked. "What did you expect me to say? That you'll be better than her at everything? One thing I've learned about women, and this ain't much, is that they're a might better at a lot of things, but not everything. They'll need you when they need you, and not when they don't. But that don't mean that they won't love you with all that they have. And keep you as safe as you'll want to keep

72

her."

"What if I can't?" He knew this was the real reason for his concern about a mate. "I'm not like the others. I don't have any idea how to shoot a gun, use a knife, or any of those things. I work for a vampire that has more going on in his life than I do. Even before he came along. Dad, she's going to think I'm an idiot."

"No one is going to think you're a sap, son, nor an idiot. They'll see you just as we all do, a moron." Tanner laughed. "See, that's why she'll love you. You know when I'm having fun with you. And any woman that comes along to find you, she won't find you lacking, Tanner, but the best thing since sliced bread. Like we all do."

"I didn't say she'd fine me lacking, Dad. Just not gooey or sappy." They both laughed then; it was better now, he'd bet. "My house, it's almost done. What if she hates it? I mean the fact that she can change it with just a thought. Or something, I don't know."

"Then she does. Not that big of a deal, is it, if you found yourself someplace that you both love? I mean, when you bought that thing, you didn't care much for it, did you? I'm thinking that not much has changed." He shook his head. "See, you might want to sell it, or just rent it out to one of them big wigs that are in town for the business meetings. Or something like that. Don't go looking for trouble, Tanner, until it's slapping you around. And think of this…when she does show up, you'll be better prepared for her."

"How do you figure that?" He told him. "I have been taking notes on things not to do with a mate. The only one I can see that has done a fine job of it right from the start is Randal. He just eased into his relationship without any kind of trouble."

"Yes, but trouble is coming. Today, I heard." Tanner nodded and asked him if they were ready. "As ready as we can be about the unknown. Me? I'm going to enjoy watching that pretty little wife of Randal's give her stepmom and dad the slapping around that they need. It's a shame it has to be right after Christmas, but that'll give us more to be thankful for in the New Year. A new beginning."

"Then Noelle will have her baby soon after, then a few months later, Marty will too. Do you think that Laney or Chloe will be breeding soon too?" TJ said that he hoped so. "Yes, me too. I love being an uncle."

When he stood, so did TJ. He was going to have another cup of tea and some of those biscuits that had been brought over for him. He had a feeling that this son wasn't the last one he'd see today, and he was going to fortify himself for it. Laughing, he was pouring his tea when his own mate came into the kitchen.

"You giving those boys trouble or advice?" He said a little of both. "Good. Tanner wanted to see you. Has he been by?"

"He has and gone now. Did you need him?" She smiled at him. "He's upset that his mate is lurking about."

"Lurking? Good heavens. What does he expect her to do, jump on him or something?" TJ hugged his wife to him after setting down another mug for her too. "You and I, we have our work cut out for us, don't we?"

"Yes, and I'd not have it any other way." She laid her head on his chest and he told her he loved her. "You're the best thing that has ever happened to me."

"And you me. Then we had to go and ruin it all by having six boys." She looked up at him with a smile. "I'd not change that either. Would you?"

"Never."

~~~

Lance was chilled to the bone. He'd forgotten how cold winters could be in Ohio. The one other time he'd been here had been more than enough for him. Damn it all to hell, he wished they'd stayed home until it was warmer. But they had to get there before all the work they'd done so far was for nothing, whatever that was. Rosemarie had a plan, and he hoped it was done soon. He still wondered why Rosemarie's little girl, Sally Anne, had moved here in the first place. He asked Rosemarie.

"She said that she had someone that could help her get on the welfare here. And then she fell in love. I guess love don't care where you go or live so long as it's together. And they were happy, don't you think?" He agreed. "I'm going to miss her so much."

"Me too." He thought of his own daughter again, and how she had cut ties with him long ago. Like she didn't want him to be happy, live his life the way he wanted. She was forever complaining about his lifestyle and his friends. He supposed that she had a lot to be complaining about. He had gone off the road a few times, and it worried him that it would catch up to him soon.

"I guess we'll just have to write Laney off as helping us very much. I only think she sent money to my baby that one time, and then nothing. I don't know what her problem was." Lance said he didn't know.

But he did. Laney had pointed out to him on numerous occasions how he wasn't the man that she knew, and that her mom was more than likely rolling over in her grave on the things that he'd been up to. Rosemarie had pointed out that she was jealous, that Laney couldn't stand for anyone to have any fun if she wasn't involved. Lance had thought that was right, but the more he thought about her, the more he was concerned for his own selfishness. Or that of Rosemarie. How could she want so much from Laney when there was so many things they could get for free if they wanted it? To him, when a family member needed help, it was because they had nothing more they could do for themselves. Rosemarie and Sally Anne wanted everything handed to them. Him too, he supposed. But of late, he'd been thinking that was wrong too.

But there was more to it than that. He'd done a few illegal things, like stealing those little babies. But they'd made sure that they were in better homes, hadn't they? Rosemarie had told him that she'd had each and every one of the people that they sold the kids to investigated, and they were as clean as a whistle. Of course, there weren't many that would see it their way, he knew this. But to him, they'd been doing a service. Not just for the kids, but the welfare department too. They no longer had to worry about having to feed those little guys.

"You ready to figure this shit out?" He asked her what she meant. "I gotta go to the funeral home that is mentioned in the paper and see about making sure she got the best of care. Her and Clay. It's gonna be hard on me, I know that, but I have to do it. You wanna go with me?"

"I do. You might need me to hold you should it prove too much for you. I can't imagine how painful this might be for you to lose a daughter. I know that even though I never see Laney, it would kill me to have her die so young." Rosemarie nodded. "You think they did anything to make sure that we were coming to see her off? You did tell them we were coming, didn't you?"

"They didn't. I don't know why just yet, but I aim to find out why. I mean, she's my little girl, ain't she?" He agreed as he pulled on his coat. The hotel they were staying in was cheap, but it mattered little. They had no intentions of paying up anyway, Rosemarie told him. They'd get compensated for it when the funeral arrangements were sorted out. He had no idea what that meant, but he believed her. Sort of.

While that bothered him at times, the way they stole and skipped out on things, he didn't let himself lose any sleep over it. As far as he was concerned, the state would reimburse the hotel for it. And it wasn't like they took the towels or anything when they left. They might have to make up a bed or two, and that would be the end of it. Neither he nor Rosemarie smoked anything in the room, nor did they mess up. It was a no brainer for the hotel to just write it off, Rosemarie told him. That brought up something else that he'd been thinking on.

She knew a lot of things like that. He didn't of course, being that he'd lived a life free of crime, or getting into trouble for anything. Rosemarie not only knew what the consequences would be if they were caught, but how to jump through loopholes so that they didn't. That bothered him more than just a little bit.

They walked to the funeral home. He was amazed at how beautiful the snow looked for being so fucking cold. He looked at the Christmas sales going on too, and had forgotten that yesterday was the big holiday. Not that he had the funds for anything special. They just enjoyed life, and that was enough for Rosemarie, she'd told him. But he did miss Christmas mornings with his wife and daughter. When she'd been tiny, he'd light up when she sat at the tree and opened her gifts.

"How about when we talk to Laney, we see if we can meet her at a restaurant that might serve up some steaks? We might as well get as much as we can out of her while she's around." Rosemarie thought that was a brilliant idea. He just wanted to see her. Maybe get a hug or two from her. "Maybe she'll have her old man a gift or two. Something that we can take back for the cash, of course. Or some gift cards. I'd like that too."

He didn't have anything for her, but he thought under the circumstances she'd understand. They'd not been on the best of terms of late, and he'd not had the funds to spend on her. He had himself a habit. He was not a drunk, but had a habit of having a drink or two a day, and that took up a lot of their cash. Lance supposed he could have gotten her something, but why? She had a job and he didn't. But that wasn't it either, and he knew it in his heart. He didn't know her well enough to buy her even stationary should she want any.

The funeral home was the nice kind, where the carpet was only in a few places and hardwood floors were in the rest of the building. He and Rosemarie were shown to a lovely room, but there was free coffee but no donuts, and that sort of depressed him. He was hungry, as they didn't have any way to eat in the big room without money. Lance thought of pancakes and sausage links, and his belly growled in protest of the meal not there for him.

The man in a dark suit joined them just as he was trying to figure out a way to take the creamers with them. The ones at the hotel were those powdery kind, and this was milk. Well, milk-like stuff.

"Hello. I'm sorry that I wasn't here to greet you, but we didn't know you were planning to come in." Rosemarie explained to him that they'd only just gotten in. "The funeral was a few days ago, as I'm sure you're aware. The two of them had a great many visitors, and the flowers filled a van up when we took them out to the cemetery."

"Only one van load? As well liked as they both were, I thought there would be a lot more. We'll take them when we go." He looked confused. "The flowers. We'll take them when we go back to the hotel with us. I mean, we walked here, so it would be nice if you could have the van just bring them out to the hotel for us. And if there are any planters, we'll have to have those too. Just as a memory of her and the funeral that no one waited on us to be here for."

"I'm sorry, miss, but they've been delivered to the Calhoun household. Like I mentioned before, we had no way of knowing that you'd be coming. Along with the flowers, the book was taken, as well as any well-wishers that were sent here as well." Rosemarie asked why they'd have them. "Well, it was my understanding that your daughter made all the arrangements and that she'd be getting her flowers and such. So, we took—"

"Not my daughter. You buried mine. That would be his. What is she doing with these Calhoun people anyway? I didn't think she lived around here." Lance said that she was living in Vegas and as far as he knew, didn't know anyone here. "Where are these people? And what do we have to do to get my things from them?"

"Mr. and Mrs. Calhoun paid for the services. As well as the burial plots and flower arrangements. There was a reception back at Randal's mother's home, but that was paid for by them as well. I'm sorry." Lance was so confused about this that he looked at Rosemarie and asked her if she knew them. She, of course, was on a roll now, and too pissed off to question her about anything. But the director seemed to understand what they wanted to know. "They're the town leaders. A very wealthy and well-respected family. I think they might have been the first family that was settled here. I know that Tanner is a fine attorney, and that—"

"Who cares? That does not explain to me why they got my daughter and her dearly departed husband's things. And where is my granddaughter? I'd very much like to see her too, so that I can make arrangements to take her back with us." The man had that look again, like he was mad but not letting his temper get the better of him. Pinched too, like he was holding in a fart that he wasn't sure he could make quiet. "Well? What the fuck are you doing just sitting there? I want my things, and my granddaughter. I'd hate to call the police on you for giving things away that you had absolutely no rights to."

"All right. Let me make a couple of phone calls, and I'll see about getting someone down here to talk to you about what you are claiming has been taken from you." She told him it had been. "I'll return shortly."

Just as the man was leaving, he reached over and took the creamers. All of them, so that Lance would not even have any for his own cup. Damn it all to hell and back. If the pot hadn't been so hot the man would probably see about taking it from the place too, he'd bet. There was no call for him to be like that. It was only creamers. It was not like he didn't get a tax break for having it around.

"Sometimes you just have to get a little loud to get what you want. The nerve of these people taking shit that don't belong to them. I don't care if they did pay for everything.

There wasn't any need for them to take the flowers and shit. We could sell off the vases if they're nice ones, you know. And maybe even a few of the flowers it they're still in good shape. Without those cards we had to pay for gas and shit, so we're going to need a little extra for the trip home. Laney must have found out about them and canceled them again." She snapped her fingers. "I forgot to ask him where Laney was staying. I thought she'd be at that hotel, but that guy wouldn't tell me. I'll ask him when he gets back in here."

"Did you see that he took the creamers? How childish is that? I wasn't going to take the cup they were in, just the little things. The coffee is so much better when it's milk and not that powder stuff." She said she'd make sure he had some after this meeting. "You're so good to me. I think that's why I like you so much."

He couldn't say it. Not for the last few days could he make himself say those three little words to her. He didn't love her...Lance was sure of that. There might have been a time when he had, but no longer. And he wasn't even sure what had brought this thought process to him.

"And I love you."

The man returned and said that he'd put out a call, and that Mr. and Mrs. Calhoun would be in shortly. She asked about where Laney was staying.

"I'm sorry, but I don't know who that might be. There have been a lot of people in and out of here lately, and she might have been in and I didn't notice her." He said if they'd wait here, they couple would be in shortly.

"You can bring back the creamers that you took from here too. When you offer coffee to someone, then you got to expect them to have cream." He said that he thought those were spoiled. "Then you make good on them. I'd like a tea too, with a shot of bourbon if you have it."

"I do not." He sounded so indignant that Lance laughed. "I don't know what sort of establishment you think this is, but we do not have a bar that you can lean up to."

When he left them, they both had a good laugh about it. The creamers were brought back, but there were only three this time and not a whole bowl of them. He took them anyway. And the girl, this time, said that there wasn't any tea to brew for anyone, but that she could being some hot water in if Rosemarie had a tea bag. That didn't go over well either.

"Do I look like I have a grocery store on my back? Where the hell would I carry around tea bags at? Mother fuck. Just go on down to the store and get some. What's the big deal? I want a cup of tea." The younger woman just left them without saying whether or not she was coming back. Lance didn't care. It had been fun, for a few minutes anyway.

They were sitting there about twenty minutes when the door opened behind them. Lance just glanced at the door, having too much fun looking around the office. It was a really nice one, and made him miss his own way back when he had a house. But then he looked back, really hard. He knew her, the woman that was next to the big man, but couldn't place her. It wasn't until she spoke that he felt his world sort of shift around. All in the wrong directions.

"Hello, Dad. Rosemarie. They said you have some issues about Sally Anne's funeral arrangements." Rosemarie stood up and walked to his daughter. When she drew back her hand, to no doubt hit her, Laney spoke again. "Do it, and I swear to you that you're going to be walking away with one less appendage."

CHAPTER 6

Randal sat at one end of the large conference table, his brother Tanner to his right and Laney to his left. Her father and stepmother sat on the other side of the table, but looked no less out of place for being side-by-side. Tanner had been with them when the frantic director had called. Mr. Patter wasn't used to being spoken to the way he had been. But once he was calmed down, Tanner suggested that he go, in the event they tried something else. The larger room was given to them, because Tanner asked for one that was as far from the public as they could get. Mr. Patter was more than happy to help out.

Tanner winked at Laney and started handing out paperwork. "This is the copy of the bill for the double funeral for the Zenicks. Also, you'll note that there is a fee for calling hours, as well as flowers for the caskets, that is there as well." He cleared his throat before continuing. "There wasn't an open casket for either of them. They were not found until six weeks after they passed, so it was better not to have a viewing. There were calling hours, but not an open viewing."

"Where are they buried? And why didn't someone wait on us to get here? Laney got here damned quick. You couldn't have waited a few more days?" Tanner said that due to the shape the bodies were in, there wasn't any way to hold off any longer. "All right, I can see that. Where are her things?"

"Things?" Tanner had a list of the items that were left in the house, but all of that had to be burned. He explained that to her. "There was nothing left. It had to be dealt with by a firm that deals in that sort of thing. As you can imagine, there was a very bad odor in the house that lingered in the things in the bedroom where they were found. I'm sorry."

"No pictures of her? You know, after they were found? How do I know that you even have the right person?" Randal squeezed Laney's hand when she looked as if she was going to speak. They'd been told not to speak unless spoken to. He thought that was going to be sooner rather than later, the way her dad kept staring at her.

"The coroner might have taken pictures during the autopsy, but we can't get a copy of those, I'm sorry. As for any pictures in the home, no, there was nothing left there that could be salvaged except a couch or chair, I think. The stove and refrigerator that belongs to the landlord, but I think once he has to go in and clean it up, those things will be taken out as well." Randal kept waiting for them to ask after Heather, but they seemed more interested in what they could get. "As for the floral arrangements that were sent to the funeral home, those too have been dealt with. The planters, which there were several, were sent to the local nursing home for those people to enjoy. Any other arrangements were also given to the local hospital to freshen up some rooms."

"You had no right to just give my daughter's things away.

I want you to go and collect them back and give them to us."
Tanner simply said no. "What do you mean, no? No, you're
not going to go get them? Or no, we have no right to them?
She was my little girl."

"Yes, she was. But the funeral and all the arrangements
were made by someone else, and paid for too. Since there was
no will other than a handwritten note about one or two things,
nor any insurance, then someone had to pay for it. If you'd
like, I can have someone send you a bill for half of what was
taken care of. That way, I can make sure you are compensated
for half of whatever flowers were given away."

"You fucking ass. I want my daughter's things. She's
gone and I got nothing, not one thing to remember her by.
And now you're trying to stick me with half the bill. What
sort of monster are you, anyway? Who paid for this, anyway?
I'd like to tell them thanks for nothing."

"I paid for it." No one spoke when Laney did. "My
husband and I paid for everything. Also took care of some of
their unpaid bills that had mounted up. They were using their
food card for drugs, and there wasn't anything left for things
like food and the electric bill. It's all taken care of."

"Husband?" Her dad stood, then sat back down. He
looked at Randal, then back at Laney when neither of them
said anything. "You're married? To this man? When did that
take place? Why didn't you tell me?"

"Tell you what, Dad? That I met someone that is nothing
like you and loves me? Or did you want to hear that I've
fallen madly in love with someone and he's kind and good to
me? So is his family, if you want to know. They're the nicest
people I have ever been in contact with." He said that he was
her family. "No, you stopped being my family the first time

you were arrested for drunken conduct in a public setting. If you'll remember, that was the day you came to my school to get me out early so I could drive you to the store to get more booze. Right around the time that you hooked up with Rosemarie. Correct?"

Last night Laney had told Randal everything. How her father had met Rosemarie at a bar one night when he'd been there drowning his sorrows. Then not a week later, they were married, her dad told her, and they became a blended family. But she was the only one that hadn't blended. Laney had been the outcast from the first day, and she stayed that way. Joe and Chloe had provided the rest.

There were arrest records for all three of them, including Sally Anne. For some of them she'd only been a minor, but after a while they put her name with her parents' as trouble too. As soon as she was able, Laney had left home and had found her own way. Sally Anne had moved to Ohio, and her dad and Rosemarie had moved to Florida, where she said that she was glad they were, and not bothering her.

"Why do I care how this was paid or by who? I don't, in case anyone cares. I want to know where my daughter's things are that were given to her as gifts when she died." Laney said that there were none, just the flowers. "You expect me to believe that nobody sent a single meat tray, or even a little bit of cash to help out with the arrangements? I don't, in case you were wondering."

"I don't really care what you believe or not, Rosemarie. She's dead, along with her drug addict husband. What you might want to think about is how Heather is taking this. How she lived in that house for six weeks with their dead bodies rotting in the other room. That she had to go in there and take some cash from Clay's pocket so she could have food in her belly." Her father asked where she was now. "At our home. As far away from the two of you as I can make her."

"That's my granddaughter, and you'll bring her to me this minute. And I'm taking her back with me when I go too." Laney stood up and so did he as Rosemarie continued. Tanner stayed put, but he was watching the couple as closely as Randal was. "You think to keep her from me? My own granddaughter, when she needs me?"

"Yes, as a matter of fact, that is exactly what I'm going to do. And we both know that she's no more your granddaughter than I'm your child. She's your little girl, my father's and yours." Rosemarie denied it. "Deny it all you want, but Sally Anne never had a child that lived past birth. She never was able to carry a child to term because of the way her body was poisoned by drugs. It's your child, and we have proof."

Rosemarie said that they had no such thing. And when a sheet of paper was laid before her, she picked it up then handed it to Lance. Until that moment, Randal had no idea that the woman couldn't read well, if at all.

"It's her birth certificate. It has both our names on it. And now that I look this over, I'm seeing that she might not be my child at all. Rosemarie, is that right?" Rosemarie told him that Heather might not be, but said that wasn't the point. "Then what is the point? Is she mine or not? I think, after all this time, I should know that. Not that it matters a hill of beans to me about her, but it would be nice to know what you did behind my back, don't you think?"

They left then. Laney had had enough, and he could feel her hurt. As they were leaving, he heard her father demanding again to be told if Heather was the father. Tanner said he'd finish up, but Randal wasn't sure what it would be about when Rosemarie was as single minded as he'd ever seen.

Laney left him there as she ran to the ladies' room and he waited. Mr. Patter came to stand with him.

"They're not nice people." He said that they were not. "I'm sorry to have called you in about this, Randal, but I didn't know what else to do. They were threatening me with the police. And even though we've done nothing wrong, you just don't want the police in front of a funeral home. Not the way tongues will wag about nothing."

"You did the right thing. Don't worry over it. My wife and I will deal with them if they threaten you again." He asked about Laney's first name. "Yes, that's her. I guess when we were here for the funeral we didn't mention that, and I'm sorry about that."

"They were so upset with me. Like I'd stolen all their worldly possessions. They didn't have any from what I'm to understand." Randal said that they didn't. "I hate to say this, but I cannot believe that your pretty young wife is related to those people. They were stealing the creamers that I put in my tea."

"I'm so sorry."

Laney came out of the bathroom then, a little pale, but he knew she was all right. He told her what Mr. Patter said. Laney told him she was sorry as well, and he told her not to worry. But he was glad that the funeral was over before they got here.

"Not to say that I did it on purpose, mind you, but I think they would have been a great deal of trouble anyway. They asked me for liquor, like I have some sort of license for something like that. I never. I just never." Laney nodded and told him that they were both drunks, and would be dealt with soon enough. "If you don't mind me saying, miss, I'd not let them near me again. I don't think they're right in the head. I'm sorry, but that's the way I feel about them."

"You don't have to worry about me, Mr. Patter. The Calhouns are taking very good care of me." Laney said she was ready and they headed for the door.

Randal could hear yelling from the general area of the room they'd just left with her parents there, and wondered how Tanner was holding up. Reaching out to him, he made sure he was going to be safe there with them before they left.

They're a trip, I'll tell you that. The mister is sort of in shock, I think. One, because we knew about the child and he didn't. And secondly, I think he's never seen his daughter in this sort of light before. Randal asked him what he meant. *A grown up. Married grown up. He keeps saying things like she was pretty, and that she was all grown up. Do you know how long they'll be around before being arrested?*

Anastasia said that it would be a couple of days. She wants them to get into trouble here. And there is no doubt whatsoever that they will. At least she will, even if it's to hit someone. They've been getting into things since they left home. Also, Chloe has been in touch with a couple of agencies down there, and they're sending someone here to issue some arrest records that are outstanding on them both. I forgot to tell you that this morning.

She told me, and sent me copies of what they were going to do. Is Laney all right? He said she'd been sick before, but he thought she was going to be fine. *I cannot imagine what is going through her head right now. The poor thing. I'm going to call in the family when I get home —*

The silence was scary, and Randal had a feeling that one

or both of them had hit his brother. *Tanner?* He told him to wait a moment. *Tanner, I'm coming up there. Are you all right?*

Yes. I'm all right. But I think her father is having a heart attack. I've called 911.

Randal told Laney what was going on, and she didn't move out of the car that they'd been getting into.

"Do you think I should go back in?" He said it was up to her. "I can't believe how I feel right now, Randal. I just don't care."

"Understandable." He did understand too. More than she might think he did. "We can go on home and wait for a call, or follow the ambulance to the hospital. Whatever you want to do."

"Follow them. I think if I were to go in there now, Rosemarie would blame me for this. And it would get nasty." Randal thought she was correct in that. "If you don't mind, can you contact your family and let them know? Not Heather. She doesn't need to know any of this is going on, if we can help it."

Randal let his family know what had happened and what they were doing. His mom was upset that they'd treated her daughter that way, and Joe was spitting mad. Not at him or Laney, but at the Prices. His dad and grandda said they'd meet them at the hospital with Trent, as they were in town already. Randal thought that would make Laney feel better.

~~~

Laney wasn't sure what she was supposed to do. She wasn't worried that he'd die. The doctor had assured her that it wasn't a heart attack, but simple heartburn. Plus a little stress on top of that. As they sat there waiting for some word on whether or not they were going to keep him, she thought of her father.

He'd been such a good man before her mom had died. Dad had told her once when she'd been called to send money that he'd been stifled with her mom. That he'd not been able to live until he'd met Rosemarie. Laney asked him if his reason for being able to live was to make her life miserable, and he'd laughed.

"You're miserable because you don't want to live. Do you see the correlation here? You're stifled too. But unlike me, you've kept on being that way instead of letting off steam. I'm having a good time. Can't you be happy for me?" She told him she couldn't. "See, that's what I'm trying to tell you. You're not living."

"Dad, I have a good job that I'm very good at. I have a roof over my head all the time, and I pay my bills when they come due." She'd not mentioned that she had a savings account, sure that they'd figure out a way to get to it too. "You're living on welfare, you don't have a job nor a decent place to live. And you're drinking a great deal."

"I get drunk too, a lot." She asked him why he'd do that. "Because I can. Don't you understand? When I was living with your mom I was a good man. I did everything I was supposed to do. And then when she died, it was as if my whole world was gone too. That I had nothing left in me. I wanted to die too."

"So did I, but I didn't go out and marry the first person that came along. I didn't drink myself into a stupor every night. Dad, you've been getting worse and worse since I left home. When will it stop?" He told her that he would be dead before he became a man that he didn't like. "So you didn't like being my father? Husband to my mom?"

"Honestly? No, I didn't like being any of those things."

She'd hung up on him then, and never called him back. Even when he called her, leaving messages that he was in trouble, or they needed money, she never called him back. And then after sending money to Sally Anne and seeing what she'd done with the cash, Laney washed her hands of all of them. She wasn't going to be a part of their downward trend, ever.

"Laney, the doctor is coming."

She stood up and waited for him. Randal stood with her, and she felt sorry for him. There was too much going on, and she hated that he was having to be a part of it. But he loved her, and that was what was getting her through.

"Mr. and Mrs. Calhoun, I'm the doctor taking care of your father. Doctor Burt Spencer. I wanted to tell you that he's doing fine now. We're going to keep him overnight, simply as a precaution. He's slightly dehydrated, and we're giving him some fluids. Also, Rosemarie, I think her name is, is insisting that he be put into a private room where he can have peace and quiet, and I've explained to her several times that it's not necessary. Nor is it covered under the cards that they have for another state." She asked him if that went over well. "Not really, but I'm made of sterner stuff. You should be warned, however, that she's looking for you. If you confront her here, we can treat any wounds that might be inflicted on her. I've been tempted since your dad was brought in."

"I can take her." He nodded and she asked him what had caused his trouble breathing. "Stress most likely. I'm to understand that he's lost his daughter?"

"I'm his daughter. It was his stepdaughter that passed away recently. Her and her husband died of a drug overdose."

He said that made a difference in the information he could give her. "I don't understand."

"They're not married. You father and that woman. I just heard back from the hospital that had treated him before that there are no records of them being wed at all." She staggered a little, and he caught her when Randal did. "I'm sorry. I thought you might have known that."

"No. I mean, I thought all this time that they were married. And that he adopted my stepsister, Sally Anne." He said that there wasn't any record of that as well, and he'd had them check. "I see. So.... That does put a different light on things, doesn't it?"

"I'm sure it does for a lot of reasons. Not just medical, I'm afraid." The doctor laughed. "As I was saying, as his medical card doesn't cover private rooms, he won't be moved into one unless they can pay for it. And since Rosemarie stated that they have no funds, I can see where that's not going to happen."

"Thank you. I'll try and explain it to her when she finds me." He started away, then came back. "She asked you if I was paying the bill, didn't she?"

"Yes, I'm afraid so. More like she said that I was to send you the billing. I think she has it in her head that your father is dying and it's all your fault. Also, Chloe is here, and she's taking her statement now, about how you caused this and you stole from her."

"Did she happen to mention what it is she thinks I stole from her?" He told her something about flowers and meat trays. "I'll take care of her." When he left them, Laney looked at Randal. "Are you still happy that we married? I'd be running for the hills about now."

93

He kissed her on the mouth and told her that this was simply a bump in the road. His dad said that they'd had worse and that she was a trooper. Leaning against Randal as he held her, she listened as TJ told her about the time he'd been on a walk and had seen a woman digging up a grave of her mother.

"Said that she'd been buried with her jewelry. Not her mom's mind, but hers. And that the funeral home had messed up in not taking it off her." Laney asked what had happened. "She was arrested, charged with all kinds of stuff, and come to find out, there wasn't any jewelry at all. She just wanted to go in and beat her mom up for not putting her in the will. Sorry people around now days, don't you think?"

"I do." Rosemarie could be heard coming down the hall before she got to them. "I'd like to handle this, if you don't mind. But don't leave me with her."

"I will never leave you. None of us will."

TJ and James said they had her back too, and she felt better. This was going to be a showdown, she just knew it. "Hello, Rosemarie."

"Don't you go acting all high and mighty to me, young lady. I know what you are. What are you going to do about this?" She asked what she was referring to. "This hospital bill. The fact that they have him in a room with a bunch of other sick people. The least you can do is fix it so that I can stay with him and have a bed. You are the cause of him having a heart attack anyways, and you know it. With all your rules and stealing our daughter's things."

"Dad is fine where he is. There was no heart attack, but only heartburn. He's stressed, but I think that has more to do with you than me." Rosemarie asked her what she had done.

"Well, dragging him into your level of trouble for starters. Then there is the ride from Florida. I can well imagine that being with you for several hundred miles wasn't a walk in the park. Did you make him drive all the way, or did you take your turn at the wheel? And, this was a great surprise, but I know that you're not married, so don't expect to be getting any updates on his health from now on."

"You fucking cunt." Laney smiled at her. It felt good to be on the other end of her rage for a change by having the upper hand and people to support her. "You don't know fucking shit about us. You're the cause of all of this. Why, I'd bet any kind of money that you had something to do with the drugs that my daughter and her wonderful husband took."

"As I know you have no money, I'm not too terribly worried about any kinds of bets you'd be making. And if you want to know the truth, Sally Anne bought the drugs all on her own and shot up with him, so there goes her wife of the year award. Then there is the added fact that they did these things right there in the same house as your little girl. The one that you gave to the drug addicts for whatever reason."

She drew back again to hit her. This time it wasn't her that stopped her, but James. He stepped in front of her and growled low. There was fury there, and she'd not want to fuck with the man, no matter if he was sporting a lot of gray.

"In the event that you don't remember, this is my grandfather-in-law, James Calhoun. The other gentleman is my father-in-law, TJ. Better men than you've ever met, and good to me." She wrapped her arm around Randal's and smiled. "This is my husband, Randal. A man that I love more than myself. You wouldn't understand that, because you don't know how to love, to be kind, nor appreciative of what you have. I'm speaking of me. You have fucked me over enough, Rosemarie, and you don't want to try your shit on me anymore. I'm not that little girl that you locked in the closet with the lights off, and I'm certainly not the child that you tried to sell off to your friends when I was home alone with you."

"Do you hear yourself? All these lies you're telling, it's a wonder you're not struck down by a lightning bolt." She looked over at Randal. "You've made a major mistake by marrying her. I can tell you things about her that would curl your toes. She's a money grubbing monster that makes up stuff just to make herself look good. Or sad…I've not figured that out yet. But if you can, I'd just divorce her and never come back to her."

"Really? I love her. Very much, as a matter of fact. And I know things about you that will land your skinny ass in prison. And also, you should know that we're going to adopt Heather and raise her the way that she should be raised. By loving, non-addictive parents." She backed up from him when he started to get closer. "So, the next time you try and accuse her of something, you'd better be taking a long hard look at your own life. The shit that you've done, as well as what it's going to cost you now that you're caught. And you are caught, Rosemarie. Both of you are."

"I'm not afraid of you. Either of you." She lunged at Randal like she'd seen children do to try and intimidate other children. All he did was laugh. "You two are going to regret this. See if you don't. Now I'm going to go see my husband, and you aren't to come and bother him."

The nurse behind Rosemarie cleared her throat. She looked directly at her and smiled when Laney asked her if she

96

could help. Nodding, she took a step closer to her and told her what was going on.

"Your father has requested to see you and your husband, Mrs. Calhoun. Also, it's been taken care of with visitors to him. Doctor Spencer said to tell you that if you have any more troubles," she looked pointedly at Rosemarie, "that you can give him a call and he'll call in the troops for you."

"I think we'll be fine, but tell him that I'll keep that in mind." Rosemarie asked what was going on. Instead of answering her, she smiled again and felt the power of it all the way to her heart. "None of your business, and stay the fuck out of my way or I'll turn you every which way but loose."

They left her standing there, the four of them headed to her dad's room. She had no idea what he wanted, or why he'd care to see her or Randal, but right now she needed a minute. Leaning against the wall outside his room, she thought she was going to be sick again. James started laughing and she joined him. It felt pretty damned good to have the upper hand in this.

CHAPTER 7

Lance hurt. His head was pounding, his legs were shaky, and he felt like he was going to be sick again. It had been an eye opener when he'd been taken away in an ambulance. The doctor had said it hadn't been a heart attack, but there was some stress there. He had thought it was a joke, that someone was teasing him about the pain he was in, when Rosemarie had started screaming at them to make him better now.

He'd been just sitting there in the chair doing nothing but thinking. About a lot of things. It hit him then that he was an idiot. And not only that, he was lonely. Yes, he had Rosemarie, but why did he have her? It was a stupid question, he supposed, but really, why was he hanging around such a caustic person? It wasn't as if he loved her; he'd figured that out a while back. It was so against everything that he'd ever been before that it hit him hard how bad he'd fucked up.

His daughter was married. After Rosemarie started screaming about how she was going to sue them all, all he could think about was his little girl and how she'd grown up without him knowing when that had happened. He also thought of how he'd missed her. He hadn't before then, he didn't think. Of course he had thought of her…not as often as he thought he should, but he had. And then, in the blink of an eye, not only had he felt like he was going to die, but his entire life, all the good and the bad, had flashed before his eyes, and he was really saddened by it all. Because as much as he hated to admit it, even to himself, most of his life had been really terrible of late. And filled with very few, if any, good things he could be proud of.

Lance figured that his chances of making things up to his daughter were slim to zip. The things that he'd seen in his walk of memories when he thought he was dying…well, his speed racing down memory lane had made him see what a real bastard he was. And while he wasn't sure that he believed in God, or even something higher, he knew that he was never going to get to go through any pearly gates, nor was he going to get his wings. Not with the way he'd been of late.

As soon as Rosemarie had left him, he called for a nurse. Lance wasn't sure she would help him, not after the way Rosemarie had blasted them all about his health. But she said if Laney was still there, she would go and give her the message. His luck would be that she'd gone home without bothering to tell him how much she loved him. Or at this point, he'd even welcome her telling him what a sorry excuse for a father he'd been, as well as a slug in the face while she was at it. He needed to get busy in doing the right things.

There wasn't much chance of her telling him that she loved him either, he thought. She had, and rightly so, washed her hands of him a long time ago. And he didn't deserve her to give him any kind of chances, not even a little forgiveness. Rubbing his hand over his heart, he knew that it wasn't the thing that had brought him here, but it hurt all the same.

"Mr. Price?" He nodded at the doctor and asked him if Laney had left. "No, she was talking to Ms. Prichard when I left her. Mr. Price, I'd like to tell you what I've been told about your scans. While you didn't have a heart attack, you do have some liver damage, as well as some spots on your lungs. These could have been caused by a great many things, but I think we both know that it's due to your drinking. And there is stress, which is making you sicker than any kind of physical problems that you might have. And I'm reasonably sure that you know what those stressors are, don't you?"

"Yes, I'm positive that I know what they are. As well as I've been a drunk for a little while now." He'd never said that aloud before, and knew it to be true. "I need help."

"Yes, you do. And in helping you out, I've taken away some of your stressors. Namely, Ms. Prichard. She is not good for your health." Lance was beginning to see that too. And feel it. He asked the doctor what he'd done. "She will no longer be permitted in your room while you're here. Since you're not married, then she has no rights to your medical history either. And because of who your daughter is and is married to, Rosemarie will be watched carefully to make sure that she doesn't set foot in my hospital again. She's upset my staff, your daughter, and a whole lot of people that are trying to help you. I'm to understand that she was arguing with Tanner Calhoun when you got short of breath and had the chest pains?"

"Yes. I was sitting there thinking of my life so far, and I realized that I'm a fool." He was glad and disappointed that he didn't disagree with him. "I'm not sure where I started on this road to no way back."

"I'd say the moment you took your first drink. And if you want to take the road back, then you're going to have to make some major changes in your life. One is drinking. That's something that will kill you just as quickly as a heart attack. While a heart attack is a quick death, drinking yourself to death? Well, it'll be slower, and you'll be in much more pain. You need to eat better. Exercise, as well as learn to say no. To a lot of people and things." He nodded, knowing that was just the start. "I can help you, Mr. Price, but all the medicine in the world isn't going to help you if you don't help yourself."

"Yes, I'd like to fix myself. At least, I'm hoping to be around for a little longer, and this was an eye opener." The doctor told him it was for many people, but few would stick to their new start, as he said he was going to do. "I will. I don't want to die. I have...I've not been the best of fathers to my daughter. Nonexistent, as a matter of fact. I want to, if I can, make a few things up to her."

"I don't know how you expect to do that when you have Ms. Prichard in your corner too." Lance nodded. Yes, thinking about Rosemarie, he knew that she had been, not totally, but some help in the relationship that he had with Laney. "But that's not part of what I'm going to do with your health. Starting today, and I mean this if you want to make changes, you're to stay on a diet. Eat better foods. I'll send in someone to tell you what those are, and have her give you menus you can start on. And exercise. You need to get out and take a walk. Get yourself a walking machine. And stop drinking. Today. Do something or you'll die. It's a simple as that."

When Doctor Spencer left him, Lance laid there and looked around the room. He wasn't really seeing it, but thinking about where he could have been had he not stressed out. Not that he wanted to go through that every time he had to rethink his life, but this was a good wakeup call. And he would make changes. He knew that if he didn't, he'd be a dead man with no one to mourn his passing, nor even realize that he was a spot on this earth. Just a stain on humanity.

If Laney came to see him—again, he doubted that she would—he was going to be strong, and he was going to tell her what an idiot he'd been. That he wanted to make changes in his life, especially between the two of them. He was also going to tell her, over and over, every day for the rest of his days, that he was sorry and that, no matter what, he loved her. That was something that neither of them said anymore to each other. And it was his fault. He'd let her and himself down a long time ago.

He was going to have to also talk to Rosemarie. That was going to be difficult as well, but he had to do it. Lance knew that he was just as responsible for his actions as she was, but he was going to stop it. Just as soon as he got out of here... before that if he could. The sooner the better, and he'd been putting it off long enough. This was going to be his time to get his life together, alone, and to make plans. Plans that he was going to follow through on. No matter the cost to himself. And he was going to make a complete confession to the crimes, all of them that he'd been a part of.

There wasn't any way that he wasn't going to go to jail. He had done some really stupid and dangerous things. And most of his life since finding Rosemarie had been illegal. Not to mention prison worthy. He also knew that even if he got life, it was no less than he deserved. He had been, in a word, stupid. For a very long time too.

As he lay there thinking, he closed his eyes. His head was

still pounding, but he was at peace. For the first time in longer than he could remember, he was relaxed enough, without the aid of liquor, to fall asleep. Before he knew it Lance was drifting off, and soon, before he could stop it, he knew that he'd fallen into a deeper sleep than he'd had in ages. It felt good, even if this was the last time he felt this good about his life, to have everything planned out like he used to.

~~~

Laney didn't want to disturb her father. She honestly didn't even want to be there at all. There was nothing he could say or do that would make her forgive him. Not just for what he'd done to her, but what he'd not done as well. Randal sat on the other side of the bed, and she thought of all the things they could be doing but sitting there with a man who, while she didn't hate, she no longer respected.

After this is done, I'm going to take you to the woods behind our house and have my wolf chase you down. And when he's had his fill of you, then I'll take mine. You are going to be so exhausted that I'm going to have to carry your naked body to the house. Where, I might add, I'm going to ravish you again. She smiled at him, but knew that her heart wasn't going to be in it until she finished with her dad. *He's talked to Burt, his doctor. Burt said that he seems to have had a change of heart on a great many things. And he wants to be healthy. Starting, he thinks, by getting rid of Rosemarie.*

I had no idea they weren't married all this time. I never really thought about it, but he told me from the start that he'd married her. I just assumed that he wouldn't lie about a thing like that. Randal told her that he might have been told to do that when they'd been married by a fake. *Perhaps, but that doesn't make it right.*

No, it doesn't. But there is a beginning here, and maybe he will do as he says. She asked Randal if he was siding with her dad.

No, I'm not. I just want you to have the right information to make a sound decision. He will be going to prison, but for how long is up to him.

What do you mean? He explained. *So if he tells on Rosemarie, he can get his sentence reduced? Do you think he'd do that?*

I don't know. I haven't any idea what sort of information he has. But Chloe told me that they do need more on her, and with your dad turning against her, since they're not married, it will go a long way to make sure that he doesn't go to prison for the rest of his life. She stared at the man who had for the most part made her life a living hell for the last few years. *But, as I said, it will be up to him.*

When I was a little girl, I think about five or six, he took me to the zoo. I haven't any idea why he decided the zoo was a place to break the news to me about Mom being sick. But when we got there, he was silly. Getting his face painted with me. We had lunch of pizza and pop, something that he never allowed me to have at home. Then as we were leaving, he told me that Mom had cancer, that she'd been sick for a while now and wasn't expected to live much longer. Randal told her he was sorry. *So was I. And mad at them both. For not telling me. For leaving me in the dark for so long. I thought of all the things that we could have been doing, hanging out and such, and I felt as if they'd decided not to tell me so that I couldn't be with them. I was wrong, I think, but when you're a kid, the world centers around you.*

He laughed. *Did you eventually get over being upset with them?* She told him that she had, when her mom invited her the next day to go to a tea. *My mom took me to one of those once. I promised myself never to go again.*

Yes, well, ours wasn't so great either. I hated the cookies they served, and I spilled tea on my dress. I guess I wasn't completely over my snit. She smiled at the memory. *In my head they were making up for time that would be gone from her. I suppose in a way that was what they were doing.*

You were just a child, and while I understand their thinking, it's wrong not to be so open. But who knows, I might have done the same thing if it happened to us. She said that she didn't know what she'd do either. *It's all right. I'm here for you should you need anything. So long as you know that, I think you'll be fine. And I've just realized that it's past lunch. Are you hungry, love? We could go get something and have the hospital call us if there is any change.*

I don't know what I am, to be honest. He told her again that he was sorry. *Yes, I am as well. But if you go and get something, I'll eat it. I know that I have to keep up my strength in dealing with all this.*

Randal left her for a bit, saying he was going to see about getting them something to eat and that he loved her. It had been a few hours and she *was* hungry, but had elected to stay in the room. She had no idea what her dad wanted, but she wasn't going to miss the opportunity to tell him a few things either. As she sat there, thinking about her life right now, she had to smile. It had turned out better than she ever thought it would have. Being in love was certainly better than being angry all the time.

Pulling out her phone, she started looking for a job. Randal said that she didn't need to work, which she supposed was correct. They had all kinds of money, he told her. But, like him, she needed to keep herself busy. While her phone was searching for a signal, she received a message.

I do hope you're happy with yourself. You've made it so I can't be in there with the man that I love. My husband. It had to be

Rosemarie, and Laney decided not to engage with her. *You're going to regret this, Laney. I mean it. I don't like having things taken from me.*

Laney, against her better judgement, decided that she was going to tell her like it was as well. Thinking about how to word her statement to the woman, she knew that with the threat she'd just placed against her, she had to be careful not to stoop to her level.

You took my dad away from me first. And I think you should be aware that I know that he's not your husband. He never was. She put a small smiley face in the message before sending it.

It did occur to her that Rosemarie had somehow gotten her phone number, but she didn't ask. After this was over, she'd just change her number again. At home she had a house phone for people to call her on; the cell phone had just been a convenient way to be reached by her work. And since she didn't work there any longer, it was a moot point.

He's my husband until I say differently. She could see that she was typing again, so waited her out. *And until then, you're to leave us alone. We just want our grandbaby.*

Grandbaby? The only way you're getting one of those is if Heather, who is too young, or I have one. And still, mine will not be related to you at all.

Bitch. You're barking up the wrong three. She was pretty sure she meant tree, but laughed anyway. *I'm going to take you down.*

All right. Bring it on. There was a moment when it said she was typing, but then Randal returned. She told him what was going on.

She's nuts. I heard from one of the security team that she left right after talking to you. So that's good. Laney took the thick sandwich and moaned when she took her first bite. *I have called Trent, and he's going to beef up the security around the house and grounds. At least until she leaves the area. Also, I've planned for your dad to be put up in one of the local furnished apartment buildings. They were in a hotel here, but he was sharing it with Rosemarie so I put him in this one by himself. They know not to allow her in.*

Her dad was still resting so they continued to speak through their link. She asked him about the apartment, and he told her that they owned the building so it wasn't that difficult to get him in. Laney wasn't sure that having him that close was going to be good, but he would need follow up care, Randal told her also that traveling alone right now might not be the best thing for him.

The doctor said that he was going to put him on a low salt low cholesterol diet. Just to get his weight down. Randal said that the apartment complex had a weight room, as well as some exercise equipment. *Thank you very much.*

No problem. And, like I said, he's far enough away that he can't just pop in to see you, and close enough to the downtown area that he could walk anywhere he wanted to go. Also, Mom went through some of our old things and found him a better coat, as well as some boots. I don't know if he'll wear them or not, but they're there should he want to. She thanked him again. *No need for that, love. I wanted to do this for you. Even if you don't take him back after this, at least we can say that we tried to make it better for him.*

After finishing lunch, she got up to move around. When Randal said he'd stay with him for a while, she walked into the hall. There wasn't much going on with this floor, but she wandered around until she found the nursery. When she was at home, in Vegas, a couple of days a month she'd go to the one in her town and be a snuggle mom.

Holding babies that needed a little extra gave her a little more too. Sometimes they were being adopted out by another family. Or the parents were from the prison and had to be returned after giving birth. Complications also made the babies need someone to hold them. Whatever the reason, Laney had loved that part of her volunteering. However, she was surprised when she saw Jas there, rocking a little one while feeding her.

"I come here sometimes, just when I need a little quiet time. Come, join me. They have two babies that need some loving." Laney was gowned up and given instructions. "They need more of our kind, people that just come in for a few hours a day." She told Jas how she'd done it at home. "Good. I was going to put your name on the list of people to help out. They pay, just a little I think, but I turn it back over to the department to use for stuffed animals or dollies and things."

"I was just needed a few days a month. I think they have a lot of people to work with out my way." She rocked the little girl, careful of the tube and other monitors on her. Laney had been around enough to know that the baby more than likely had come from a drugged momma. "They're so tiny, aren't they?"

"Yes, but sadly they can be smaller." They rocked and cooed at the babies for a little while before Jas spoke again. "You're happy here, aren't you?"

"Yes, very much so." She rocked a bit more and wondered why she'd asked. "The weather takes some getting used to, I think. I've never been in this much snow before. Randal is going to show me how to drive in it."

"Then you're staying." Ah, she thought, that was it. Laney

nodded. "I'm so glad to hear that. I've been…well, we've all been sort of worried that you'd want to go back out there. And you know that Randal, he'd go with you."

"Yes, I gave my resignation this morning and told them that I would give up my vacation time in lieu of quitting without much notice." Jas nodded. "I was going to talk to you and James. I wondered if it would be all right with you if Heather called you Great Grandma and Great Grandda? We're going to adopt her as soon as this whole thing with my dad is done."

"We'd absolutely love that. But I have to tell you, honey, she already does. We already think of her as our grandchild. Right along with Benson and the others coming along. And you can call us your grandparents too should you want. I know you have a dad, but I have to tell you, TJ, he's busting a gut every time she calls him Grandda. Heather is older than the other grandchildren, so she's the first one to do it. He just thinks the world of her. All of us do."

"Me too. I don't know her well, but I'm working on that. Randal said that she'll have to go to another classroom now that she's going to be his daughter, but she said she's all right with that too. Because he'll be a good daddy." She shivered a little when she thought of her living with Sally Anne and Clay for so long after they were dead. "She still has nightmares about her life before, but the faeries that live in her room, they keep an eye on her."

"Randal was so heartbroken for her when he went to her home. Even Noelle, the poor thing, cried for days after that. She said that she wants to hold her all the time now, just to show her that she's loved and cared for." Laney said that she did the same thing. "But she'll be fine, I think. She's young

110

and strong. And having all of us around, even though we can be a might pushy and overwhelming, we love with all that we are."

"I've come to realize that as well." They both laughed quietly, and when her time was up with the baby, she rocked a bit more, watching Jas with her third baby. "I'd like for you to sign me up for this if, as you said, you haven't already. I would love to come in here when they need me."

"Thank you. And if you want, there are several other projects that you can help me on. Not that you don't have things to do, but the others, they're so busy with their own projects. Mostly what I need is for you to help me with things to raise money for the shelter and such. We start the day after Christmas, believe it or not, in gathering things for the next one. And the food pantry could use some help as well. I'd keep you busy as my helper."

"I'd love that. I'm very organized and good with people." She said that she knew that too. "I was thinking about some of the things you do for fundraisers. Randal told me that you have one for school supplies every year. How about a casino night? I could help you with that." Jas said she loved the idea. "It'll take some work, but I think it'll be fun for the parents and kids alike. We did it once back home, and it raised quite a bit of money for the underprivileged children."

"Oh my yes, I can see it now. Yes, you and I are going to do well together." The nurse came to get the baby and they sat there for several more minutes going over their plans. "Are you sure you don't mind helping an old woman out?"

"I'm not sure. I don't know any old women, do you?" They were laughing when they came out of the little room that they'd been in. "Thank you, Grandma. I think I needed this more than I thought."

After a tight hug, she made her way back to the room. Randal was just coming out when she got there, and he held her and kissed her. He told her that her dad was awake and that the dietician was there talking to him. After telling her that he had to get to Trent's for a little while, she told him to be careful. Another tight, loving hug and she was standing there all alone. Christ, to have to go in this room was going to make her sad.

The door was already ajar when she pushed it open. The nurse with her dad was talking about what he could and couldn't eat now, as well as setting him up with someone to help him with the alcohol. He was going to be in for a long hard road doing all this at one time. She waited, not wanting to intrude while he asked her questions that surprised her.

"I'm not much of a salad eater, to be honest, but I'm going to do it. Also, can you tell me how to dress them up? You know, what kind of things I can add to it so it's fresher?" She told him no donuts, and they both laughed. "No, no more donuts for me. Nor bread like I was eating. But you know, I've heard of Cobb salad and stuff. What can I do like that?"

"Most anything you put on a salad just adds calories. You can do it, like I told you, but you have to learn to read what you're putting in your body as well as how much of it. Moderation. I told you how to make that work." Her dad must have agreed because she asked him to say it.

"Make our dinner eatable, regular, and tasty if our numbers are too high. Moderation." It took her a moment to realize that he had spelled out the word. She smiled when the nurse told him that if he remembered that with everything he put in his cart from now on, he'd be fine. "I hope so. I have

112

myself a lot of time to make up for."

She had no idea what he meant, but waited until the nurse was gone before she stepped around the curtain. Laney didn't know what she had expected from her dad, but for him to burst into tears and beg her to forgive him was not it. He sobbed and talked all over himself as he told her over and over how sorry he was, and that he loved her. Laney cried as well. She didn't know how long this would last, but for now, she had him back.

CHAPTER 8

Rosemarie hated Laney…always had, since the first time that she saw her. But she'd barked up the wrong tree with her this time, and she was going to make sure that she paid. And when she was finished with the bitch, nobody would ever know it was the same person. She was going to mess Laney up. But first, she had to get her attention.

The yard that she'd broken into was bigger than her entire floor at the place they were staying. And that had five other apartments in it. Sneaking through the trees, she was careful where she stepped. Rosemarie was going to make them all pay.

She heard her before she saw her. The part of the yard she was in was huge, and there wasn't anyone around that she could see. Someone had shoveled the walkway and surrounding area where Heather was playing. She thought that they had put her out of the house — that's what she would do with the brat — but she was only building a snowman. And seemed to be enjoying herself.

Rosemarie watched her for a little while, making sure that

there wasn't some asshole adult around that would mess up her plans. And she had a good one too…take the kid, demand some money, then kill her and Laney. She didn't want any reminders around that she'd been caught.

Having the baby had given her and Lance a few extra bucks every month. She didn't use it the way that they had intended, like buying more food for herself and shit. Her and Lance had gotten more liquor and some mighty fine things by selling off the card when they got it.

Now that she remembered on it, Lance had been kind of squeamish about that part too, knowing that it should have gone to the kid. He'd always been soft in the head as far as she was concerned now that she had gotten away from him. The little fucker was going to rue the day that he'd messed with her. And he'd loved Heather when she was with them. That was when Rosemarie had started to really hate the kid.

Then Sally Anne had come to get her, telling her that she had a buyer for the kid. It would have been good had she sold her, like she said, but her idea about scamming the county agencies was better. They had the best of both worlds. Her Sally Anne, she was sure smart about the government shit that they could get.

Seeing that nobody seemed to care that the kid was outside, Rosemarie got closer to her. She was singing some stupid tune that she probably heard in the school. The noise that she was making covered any sound that Rosemarie was making as she walked to her. When there was a pause in her racket, Rosemarie said her name. The moment she looked at her, she knew why her daughter had kept her. She was a beauty. And looked just like her little girl, Sally Anne.

"Hi." Heather smiled at her. "I'm your grandma.

Rosemarie. I was sent to take you to see your grandpa. He's in the hospital. They wanted me to come and get you to take you there."

"No." Rosemarie seldom lost her temper, but that single word could make her see red faster than anything. "I don't know who you are, and my grandma and grandpa aren't going to be happy with you if you say a lie again. You're not my grandma. I know who she is. Unless you're the bad one. Are you?"

Rosemarie wondered what they were telling the brat about her that would make her think she was a bad person. Smiling to herself, she thought of all the things she had done, even in the last month, that nobody knew about that would get her labeled like that. But she decided, for now, to ignore her comments about that.

"I don't lie. Not all the time. But this is the truth. He's in the hospital. They think he might die." Heather shook her head no and backed away from her. "Come on now, kid. I need you to come with me. It's important, so stop fucking around and get your ass over here."

"No. I know who you are. You're my mom's mom, the bad grandma. And she told me that you were a liar and a thief. She said that you'd steal money off of a dead man." Well, that was news to her. True, but hurtful too that her daughter would say something like that to her own flesh and blood. "I'm not going anywhere with you."

"Yes, you are." She was close enough now to grab the kid, and did. When she struggled to get away, she hit her with the little shovel that was lying next to the stupid snowman. When she fell to the ground, blood started to stain the snow. Rosemarie thought it was the most beautiful thing she'd ever seen.

Grabbing her up in her arms, she put a bunch of snow over her wound so she'd not get any of the shit on her clothes. Her head was bleeding pretty good by then, but Rosemarie knew that head wounds would bleed like you cut yourself in the throat. Walking away, she realized that she was leaving them a nice trail to follow, and tried to think what to do. The road…she needed to get to the road.

Walking with the kid was hard work. Rosemarie had to stop several times just to catch her breath. But she had her now, and things were going to go her way for a change. She'd have to think about the things the kid had told her when she'd talked about Sally Anne, but for now, she had to hide away and make sure that the kid was tied up.

Tying the kid up was important. Rosemarie wanted the kid all done up when she sent a picture to Laney. She'd know then that she meant what she'd said about messing with her. And she'd pay attention to her when she made her demands. And Rosemarie had a lot of them now.

First of all she was going to get Lance out of the way. She didn't want him anymore, but Rosemarie didn't want Laney to have him either. This was war, and she wasn't one to come out anyplace but at the top. She'd be the one that discarded Lance, not have him taken from her. But Lance had worn out his welcome and she was going to mess him up too. Dead was going to be her way of getting rid of baggage she no longer needed. She'd done it before, so this was old hat, she thought to herself.

It took her an hour to get to the main road. There she had to lay the kid down and rest. She had no idea that kidnapping was going to be such hard work or she might have waited until she had her car. But it was a done deal now and she'd have to move on. Planning better might have been a better way to go with this. Or to have muscles. That's what Lance had been for. Damn it all to fuck and back, she missed his brawn. He had no brain, but he sure had the other.

The car was in the parking lot to the hotel where they had been staying. Lucky for her the place had been shoveled of all the recent snow or she might not have ever gotten out. As it was, she had to make several trips back and forth to the room to get her things. And Lance's. She wasn't going to leave his shit behind just because he'd been taken from her.

Rosemarie didn't drive well. Mostly never if she could have someone cart her around. Her eyesight wasn't that good, and she would get nervous. Taking out the last bottle of booze that they'd taken, she drank down half of it before she found her courage to start the engine. The kid hadn't so much as made a sound since she'd picked her up. Not that it worried her none. She was going to die anyway, so it wasn't hurting her any to have her quiet.

Rosemarie didn't know the town well, but she had been looking around when she was out. The house that her daughter had died in was all locked up, but she knew that it was as safe a place as any to hide out until she was rested up and dealt with the brat. But she had to get there, and that wasn't going to be easy. Drinking while she drove in the direction she thought it was, she thought about the things she was going to demand she get for the kid. Plus there was the list she had in her head of rules that Laney was going to follow. Laney liked rules, so Rosemarie was sure that she'd be thrilled that Rosemarie had some. Laughing out loud made her feel much better about her driving.

119

The list of things she was going to make happen for her was long, but she thought of what she was also going to do once she was free of Lance. He'd been fun and she had loved him, but he'd dropped her like a hot potato and that just didn't set well with her. No way, no how.

There was going to be a house. Not one of them government jobs either, but one of her own. And she'd have nice things in it too. A coffee machine that had one of them timers on it so it was hot and ready when she rolled out of bed. She'd have a nice kitchen to eat in. Rosemarie didn't cook, that was for suckers, but she'd have one she could eat in, and that was what she really wanted.

A thick mattress on one of them sleigh beds, too. So many blankets to put over her that she'd have to have a map to get out. And to make that work, she wanted air conditioning. One of them suckers in every room too, set to zero so she'd never be hot again. Rosemarie hated with a passion to be hot. But not this cold either.

"Fucking weather. How the hell does anyone live here without killing themselves? It's colder than a witch's tit in a brass bra." Giggling, she knew that she'd never had the occasion to use that term before and was happy that she had. Rosemarie thought she had it right, but wasn't sure. But it worked.

After another hour of just driving around, she finally found the place her baby girl had lost her life in. There was still yellow tape around the place, but the walkways had been shoveled and there wasn't anyone around. Dropping the kid off at the doorway, sitting her up like a little doll, she took the car to a parking lot that she'd driven by a dozen times in her search and made her way back to the house.

"I'm gonna need me a nap when this is over." Laughing, she saw that the kid was just where she'd left her and shook her head. "I wonder what her dear sister would say if she saw her now. All boo-hoo, no doubt."

Wrestling her into the place after picking the lock, Rosemarie left her on the floor. The smell was horrible in the place, but nothing she couldn't handle. Going to the kitchen, she wasn't surprised to find that the cabinets were empty of all the food, and the ice box was empty too.

Nothing to eat, she pulled out the phone she'd taken from a nurse at the hospital. It was time to make some money. Snapping pictures of Heather, she made sure that there wasn't anything in them that would give away her location. Rosemarie even took a few of the wound on her head, making it bleed a little more so it would show better.

Sending it was trickier than she thought it would be, mostly because she didn't know how to use the phone. But after a little bit of playing around, she was not only able to send it out, but to type some of those little faces that Laney had sent her earlier. It was turning out to be a very good day for her.

Now she was exhausted and needed a drink. Going through the house again, this time with a mission in mind, she looked for any hooch that she could find. There had to be something here, even if it was that cooking shit that she'd drank once before. But she didn't find any booze. However, she did find their stash.

"Party time for me." She knew that to smoke weed there had to be some kind of wrapper, but all she could find was some toilet paper that had a funny odor to it, as well as some old mail. She figured that it had been delivered to the place after they'd found the bodies, because it smelled fresh rather than like ass.

Ten minutes later, she was smoking a joint. After almost setting fire to her hair and the couch, she was mellowing out. The fire had been started when the toilet paper had burned too fast, leaving drips of her fine weed to burn the couch and some of her hair. When she got them both put out, she used the paper, and again, it burned too fast, so she simply put the grass in a bowl and set fire to it. Christ, what a person had to do to get a little fun in their lives. Picking up the phone when it made a noise again, she laughed.

Laney was pissed off, it seemed, and she had sent back her own set of pictures, these of an arrest warrant, as well as some of her middle finger. She supposed it was hers, who knew. But Rosemarie didn't care. She had her attention now, and she was going to use it to the fullest.

Careful where she put her bowl, she typed up her return message. This was getting real now, and she had to be careful again not to give away her location. She didn't want her party all messed up before she got paid, now did she?

"I want money. A lot of it too. Ten thousand for the kid, and then every month I want another five grand for you to feel safe about having her unprotected." She was glad to have been able to put that little dig in there. "You should take better care of what you think of as your own, don't you think?"

The phone made another noise and she ignored it. There were more important things to get all up in arms about than a post from Laney. She thought of what she was going to say next, but the kid decided right then to wake up. Her screams could have woke up the dead.

"Shut the fuck up before I hit you again. This time I'll

kill you where you lay." Heather snapped her mouth closed but didn't stop whimpering. "You should know better than to fuck with me, kid. I'm meaner than a rattlesnake."

"I want you to take me home." She said that she was home, didn't she notice. "No, I don't want to be here. I want to be with Laney and Randal. And my grandma and grandpa. My uncles too. Uncle Trent and Uncle Elijah. And Uncle —"

"Name one more person and I will backhand you so hard you'll never wake up again." Rosemarie had a headache again. She rubbed her forehead while trying to think of a way to shut her up. The whimpering like some house dog was making her want to commit murder. But she couldn't do that until she had the money. Laney might want to speak to the kid or some shit. "Now, I want you to tell me if you know where some food is in this place. I'm hungry and I want to eat."

"I had food at Laney's house." The stubborn set of her face made Rosemarie think of Sally Anne. "I want to go home."

"Yeah, well that's not going to happen. You're with me now, kid, and the sooner you learn to listen to me the better off you're going to be. Find me some food." She just sat there and Rosemarie threatened her again. "I mean it, kid. I'm going to wallop on you something hard if you don't listen to me."

"I don't feel well." And she just leaned over and puked. "I'm sick. I think you hurt me bad."

Rosemarie could not stand someone puking. It didn't matter who it was or what they were sick over, hearing or seeing someone upchucking made her as sick as, if not sicker than, the person. Leaning over the chair she was in, she puked too. Spilled out all her guts while the kid kept telling her over and over she wasn't well. Well, fuck that shit, neither was she.

The pain to her head made her dizzy. Blinded for a few moments, Rosemarie couldn't figure out what had happened to her. There was someone in the room with her, other than the kid. Trying her best to swat at the person made her sicker still. Then she simply passed out.

~~~

"I have you." Heather didn't look all that sure of it, and Noah leaned down to her level. "Your sister Laney sent me here to find you. And since I'm a friend of hers, I will be yours as well. My name is Noah."

He had to be careful with her. The smell of blood was stronger the closer he got to her. He wasn't worried that he was going to bite her—he'd fed today—but he worried. She wasn't in good shape.

"My head really hurts." He said that he knew that it did, and when she collapsed, he picked her up in his arms and laid her across his lap. She looked at him again. "I hurt everywhere, and I can't see no more."

"I can help you." She nodded then looked to be sick again. "Don't move, child. Just trust me for a moment, will you? I'm going to give you a part of myself. That way we'll be friends for a long time."

He was running out of time, and he knew that Laney and Randal would forgive him for what he was about to do. Opening his vein, he pressed his wrist over her mouth and told her to drink. The second time, he had to command her to do so, and it tore at his heart. Reaching to Randal, he told him what he'd found.

Save her. He said that he was trying his best. *We're on our way. And Anastasia is coming to you as well. She might be able to help.*

124

The faerie would be able to help, but he knew that it was going to cost them both. As soon as she appeared in the room, as her true self, he told her what he'd found and what he was doing. Saving this child was all he could think about.

"I'll give her some of my magic as well." The blood of a faerie, given freely, would help Heather, but he was afraid they might be too late. Her heartrate was slowing and her breathing was shallow.

When the child's heartrate stopped, so did his own. She was so innocent in all this, and her life had been snuffed out by a greedy person. Just as he was ready to bundle her up, he heard the slightest flicker to her heart, then it started to beat regularly. When her eyes opened for just a second, he was startled by the color and looked at Anastasia.

"She will be well." He nodded. "I think that together we have a child, but with my blood she will become older and not remain a child for all time. We have saved her, but at a cost, I think. Not just to us, but to her as well."

He wondered about her eye color. It was no longer the dark brown that it had been. With the magic of the faerie, her eyes were now a crystal blue, almost clear in color. And they would change more now. With each year of her life, the child would gain more powers, and it would show in the color and hue of her eyes.

"They're going to be pissed off. The magic that she has, it's stronger than most have at our age." Anastasia said that they'd be happy to have the child. "I hope you're right because I'm thrilled beyond words to see her looking better."

"What will we do with the woman? We can't kill her, more's the pity. I'd like nothing better than to take her away from here and make her suffer in ways that no one will ever know." So did he, he told Anastasia. "Well, then what? The police are on their way. Should we just make it look as if she had a heart attack? It would make me feel better, but humans can be picky about what they consider justice being served."

"In this, I think she must be made to suffer at the hands of those that need it. Closure, to humans anyway, is something that they need very much." He looked over at the woman in question. "She has caused a great many people heartache, and if they cannot have this moment, then they'll suffer for it."

"And the man, the father to Laney? What do you think will happen to him?" He asked her what she meant. "Laney has confessed that she cares nothing for him. That so far as she is concerned, he is dead to her. I believe, and this is just me, I think she has only written him off because he had no desire to come to her, and in order to save her own heart, she did this to protect herself. What do you think about making him only a small part of the happenings that have transpired?"

"You can do that?" She said that she could do a great many things. "I suppose that you can. Yes, I think you might have a good idea there. It will, to me, close a lot of heartache for the two of them if he were allowed to be around. She will be glad for it, I think. Laney has a good heart. But I think, for now, we should leave here before the police arrive. The child will need to be left behind, but I'll talk to Laney and the others."

It was decided that he would stay behind in the shadows to make sure that nothing more happened with Heather. Anastasia said that she could talk to Trent, then Laney, about her father. To him, he thought the man should rot in prison for the way that he'd hurt his daughter, but Noah hadn't had a kindness in his heart for a long time when it came to humans.

As soon as the medical team entered the place with the police, he took to the skies.

You saved her. He told Randal not without a cost to the child. *Anastasia said that you both saved her and changed her. I can't thank you enough for this. Laney is happy too, but she's also upset. Her father wants to have time with her, and I think she's going to go along with him, but slowly.*

The faerie said that she could make his involvement in the deeds of the woman lessened. I didn't know what you or your mate would want, but I will help her should she need it. This would be up to Laney to decide. He said that he understood that. *If there is fallout, or he hurts her again, there will be a reckoning for him. And I do not mean a life in prison. I will hunt him down and tear him into pieces. This is a promise that I will make to him as well.*

I think you should. Noah was surprised by his consent to do this and thanked him. *No, thank you. If he is as big a fuck up as he was before, then he doesn't deserve to be in any of their lives. Thank you again.*

Randal, I don't think you're told enough how brilliant you are. Randal laughed and said it was missed a great deal. *I think that you are. And a good kind man too. I have missed that as well.*

I don't think I'm all that smart, but just a nice man. Sometimes, according to my family, a little too nice. But that's okay too. He landed near a group of men standing around a camper and wondered what they were about. It occurred to him that it was much too cold to be camping, and realized that they were fishing. An insanely boring thing to do, he thought. *Noah, they're taking her to the hospital now. I think I've had enough of hospitals for a while, how about you?*

Yes, I do believe that I have. He captured the men with his gaze, and set about taking a little from each of them. *I shall see you soon, my friend.*

When he bit into the older man, he knew the reason for the late trip. The elderly man was dying, soon too. Feeling better than he had when he arrived at the house with Heather, he decided to help this man as well. In the hearts and minds of the other men, he was a good father, a man who could be depended upon, and one that would be missed a great deal. It saddened one of the younger men that his dad would not see his son being born, nor his youngest daughter being married. He gave the man a little of himself, and took away the cancer that ate away at his lungs. There were other ailments as well, easy things that he could fix, and he did. By the time Noah left them, he needed to feed once again and found himself another group. At this rate, he'd still be trying to find himself a meal when the sun was high in the sky.

It was too late for him to go to the hospital when he was finished. Noah made his way back to his lair, his home, and settled in his living room. There was much going on in his home; a full remodel had been due for a long time. It was only in the last few months, since his Joe had found her mate, that he'd decided to stay in the area. Noah wasn't one to remain in one place for very long. But here, he thought he could.

"Sir, you have a visitor. It's the mate to Ms. Anastasia. He said that he would like to ask you a favor." Noah told Michael to let him in. "Very good. Also, I have made some refreshments for the man. He is mostly human, so I have made something that would tempt his palate."

Noah had no idea where that had come from, and was still puzzling over it when the man, Doug he thought his name was, joined him. Michael said he would return and Doug had a seat. He only sat for a moment before he stood up again and began pacing. He thought that whatever was on the man's mind, he'd spill it sooner or later.

"I should like to warn you about the refreshments that my man is bringing in." Doug paused in his walking to ask him why. "I'm not sure. He said that he was going to tempt your palate. And that you're mostly human."

"That's what I'm here for." He told him he was at his disposal. "I'm sorry that it's so late for you. Or early. I'm not sure."

"It's fine, Doug. I'm very old, and the sun doesn't bother me as much as it might someone younger. I do come home when the sun is rising simply out of habit." He didn't tell him that he had fed well and was well enough to enjoy the day, should he want to. He thought Doug was a little on edge enough for now. "What did you want to talk to me about?"

"A baby." When he said no more, Noah pointed out to him that he wasn't able to help him in that department. However, the joke went by without even a small laugh. "We're going to have a baby, Anastasia and me. She said it will be like her. Simply because of her age."

"Yes, well, she is very powerful." Doug nodded then sat down. "You don't wish a child with her?"

"I do, more than anything. But I won't see it grown." He asked him why not. "I'm going to die."

"Soon?" Again, the humor was lost on the man. "You're an immortal, Doug. All of the people that I know are. I didn't give you that gift, but you do have it. When you mate with a powerful being, such as your own mate, you are given this gift, by whatever means, so that the two of you can live on forever."

"Since when?" He said that he would imagine the first

time he was with his mate. "I see. No. I don't. Why wasn't I told this? I mean, I should have been told, don't you think?"

"Did you ask?" He said that when he thought about it, he'd get sidetracked. "Yes, well, that does happen a lot with new mates."

"I will live as long as her? You're sure?" Noah assured him that he was very sure. "Thank you. So very much. You've made my...well, I was going to say day, but I have a lot of those, don't I? To spend with my wife and children. I'm...I have no idea why I didn't ask, but I feel so much better."

When Michael joined them a few minutes later, Doug was very relaxed. And when Michael pulled a bottle of root beer from his pocket, Noah wasn't sure what to think. Then he uncovered the pizza, still steaming hot, and the pepperoni was curled up on the edges. Noah looked at Michael when he pulled three slices off the platter and put them onto a plate. Michael, of course, was all smiles.

"I have been playing with my knowledge of human food. It is most strange." Noah said that he thought so as well. "Very good. I'll be in the kitchen trying my hand at a smooth. Enjoy."

Noah started laughing when Doug told him it was a smoothie, not a smooth. Whatever it was, he thought the old boy was off his noodle a little, but fun. Noah wished he could have enjoyed a slice of the pizza. It looked very good.

CHAPTER 9

"I don't understand." Neither did she, but she waited on Anastasia to tell them again. There was too much going on, and her dad's arrest record was just a tiny part of it. Laney watched her dad as he laid there in the bed, and wanted to ask him again if he was sure that Rosemarie was out of his life. "You're telling me that if I tell you all the things we did together, you'll take my name off that record there and I'll be a free man?"

"Not free. You'll have to do some community service and some work around the town. While you'll be paid for your time, you won't be in jail. And if you're okay with that after a few months, then we'll find you something permanent." He nodded then looked at Laney as Anastasia continued. "This is a good deal for you, Lance. Not only will you be able to see your daughters, but you'll be able to stay healthy and safe. However, Rosemarie is going to prison. If only for the attempted murder of Heather."

"I didn't know she was going to do that." Anastasia said that she knew that too. He looked at Laney. There was sadness there, but she was afraid to believe that it was for her and not a ploy for her to do something for him. "Will you let me see you once in a while? I don't mean all the time. I know that I've messed up badly with you, and Heather, but I'd like to know you some. If you'll let me."

"I don't know." He nodded. Laney wasn't going to go that far with him right now. She was too hurt and too upset with both of them. "You might not have had anything to do with that woman taking Heather, but your plan all along was to take her. And to hurt her."

"Never to hurt. I mean, not in my head, no, never to hurt. And I think, now that I've stepped away from her, I'm beginning to think that a lot of things that she had me believing wasn't true." Laney nodded. "Honey, you have no idea how profoundly sorry I am about all of this. I've had a real eye opener, and I plan to make it my life's work to make it up to you."

"We'll just take this one day at a time, if you don't mind. I have a lot of hurt built up, Dad, and while I know that you're going to try, you hurt me." He said that he understood, and she could see his hurt. But this wasn't about her and him, it was about his release. "Anastasia, you're telling him that all he has to do is tell you everything that they were involved in or heard about with Rosemarie, correct? And then he won't serve any jail time? Are you sure that won't be taken from him once he starts telling you what they did? I mean, I know you're saying that now, but it could be really bad."

"Some of it is." Laney nodded at her. "Some of it would put them both in prison for all their lives. But in this, we're willing to cut a huge deal for two reasons. One, and I know you might not see it that way, but it's for you. Noah and I, and some others, think that you need a chance to have him in your life. The second reason is, we know what they did, both of them, but without help in a physical sense, she'll only get a few years for attempted murder. She'll claim, with her attorney, that she was insane at the time because her lover had been taken from her. It'll work too. No one will believe that she only did this to get back at you. They'll believe her simply because she's nuts."

Laney laughed a little and Anastasia laughed with her. Her dad, however, looked afraid. Not that she blamed him, but there was something so broken about him that she wanted to tell him it would be all right. And maybe it would, but she wasn't going to let him into her heart again only to have him stomp all over it.

"I'll do it. I'll tell you everything that you want to know. Some things you probably don't know about." Anastasia told him that she knew it all because she'd read his mind. "All right then, I'm guessing that you can ask me about it and I'll tell you. But I have to tell you now, some of it I might not be too clear on. I've been a drunk for a long time now."

"And that is why when you started to have the withdrawal symptoms, I helped you. I need to get this information now, and if I have to wait until you're clean, it'll be too late. Rosemarie will be tried on the kidnapping and that is all." He nodded and thanked her again. "You fuck me over, Lance, and not only will I give it back to you, the detox and the sickness, but I'll double it and you'll fucking die from it."

Laney left after Chloe showed up. There wasn't a lot of room in the hospital area for her and the men that were running the camera equipment, as well as the two women. She told her dad that she'd be back to take him home later, and he thanked her. Laney wanted to hug him, feel his strong arms around her again, but was afraid. Not of him, but the hurt of it. Instead, she left.

I was wondering if you'd like to meet me at the house. Laney smiled when Randal spoke to her. *I have a powerful need to see you naked, laying out over our bed while I devour you.*

You do know that I have a meeting with your mom and grandma at noon, right? He said that he told his mom that she would be late, very late. *And what did you tell her was the reason I was going to be late? Surely you didn't tell her what you just told me.*

No, God no. I told her that you and I had to talk about your father and some of the things that were going on with him. She asked him if he was in the habit of lying to his mom. *No, and she'd murder me either way, telling her the truth or the lie, so I went with the lie. I'll be able to look her in the eye.... Do you think we could not talk about my mom right now?*

She laughed. It felt good to do it, and she loved him all the more for it. *I'm on my way home now. As soon as I drop off the things at the post office.* He told her he'd be in their room. *Also, I do have one thing to ask you before you make me forget again. What about my things in Vegas? I do need to go and pick them up.*

Damn, I forgot. Trent had someone go in and pack it all up for you, and it's on its way here. He said that he would put it in one of the units that he has in town until we decide to go through it. *I'd wait for a bit. Also, he had all the food donated to the local shelter, which he said wasn't much, and your plants aren't going to survive out here so he did the same with them.* She'd have to thank him for that. *I'm naked and waiting for you.*

Christ, the things you make me feel. I have to drive there, so no more naked talk. He laughed and she told him she was not going anywhere but straight home. *You make me crazy, you know that?*

Yes, but you love me so that's all that matters. And she did. With all her heart. *Just be careful, and know that I'm right here, waiting.*

Driving home wasn't too bad, but since she was inexperienced in driving in the snow, it was hard for her to keep going. The sidewalks and streets were clear, but the slushy stuff had frozen overnight and she was a little afraid. By the time she made it home, she was not only exhausted, but on edge. Gathering her things, she made her way into the house. Heather was there waiting on her.

"I need forty-six dollars, please." She asked her for what. "There is a girl at school that needs to have a transplant, and they said it would cost forty-six dollars."

"Let me see it." When she ran to get her pad that she'd gotten for Christmas, Randal came down the stairs. She pouted at him when he shrugged.

"She came home about a minute after I talked to you. Trent said that he had an emergency with the pack or he would have kept her all day."

"I'm sorry." He said it was fine, that they'd be together for the rest of their lives. Heather came in with her little computer and showed her the article. "Honey, it says that she needs forty-six thousand. Not forty-six dollars."

She looked so disappointed that it broke her already tender heart. "I thought we could really help her. She's one of my friends I play with at recess."

Randal explained to them both that they were having the pack pay for most of it. And that the rest of it was going to be in charity donations. She wondered if that was what her meeting with the other two women was about, and decided that she would take Heather with her, to be involved.

"Well, if it's all right with you guys, I'm headed to a meeting." She kissed Randal when he pouted like she had. "I'll be back, alone, later. I'm taking Heather with me, if you don't mind."

"No. I'm sure that she might find it fun to hang out with my grandma and mom." He stood up off the step he'd been sitting on. "I'm going to find my grandda and find out what he's up to. He mentioned something about going to find a building to use for a storefront. And he wants me to look over his new camper. Then, I'd like to meet my four favorite ladies in town and take them out to dinner."

When they were in the car again, she asked Heather if she was all right. She shrugged, a sure sign that things were not okay. Laney was still nervous about what had happened to her two days ago, but for now she seemed to be just fine. But it was the extra magic, a great deal of it she'd been told, that was making her little sister a little on edge.

They had decided to keep her dad in the hospital for a few more days. Not that he was ill or anything, but they thought they'd have better control over who came to see him there. He'd been hurting when she'd arrived that morning...the shakes and the pain of withdrawal were horrendous. But with a touch from Anastasia, he not only was better but he didn't hurt any longer. Laney did wonder if he was an immortal like they were, and would have to ask. Heather sighed heavily and spoke, bringing her out of her own thoughts.

"Can I make her better?" Laney said she had no idea really what it was she could do. "If I could, I'd make sure that no kids got hurt or sick anymore. And that they got to live with people that loved them, like you and Randal do with me."

"We love you too." She said thanks, but Laney knew her sister well enough by now to know that there was more to this than just that. But she let her muddle it through before bringing it up again. Instead, she told her what they were doing. "I've decided to work with Grandma on some projects around town. They help with getting presents for the kids that might not get anything if not for them. Also, supplies for school."

"Mom did that, put me on those lists. But I never got to play with the toys and stuff. Her and Dad would take them to sell for their things." If Laney didn't hate her sister before, she certainly did more and more all the time. "And the school supplies were nice too. I got to use them, but I never had no money for fees and stuff. And I wasn't allowed to go on the trips either. Mom said it was a conpursey." She wasn't sure what that was and then it hit her.

"A conspiracy? I doubt very much that there was any sort of thing like that going on. And when the weather gets warmer, we'll go to those places you missed. All right?" Heather said she'd really like that, and asked if she could take a friend. "Of course, so long as her mom is okay with it."

"Aunt Laney, can I call you Mom? You're not really my aunt either, but that's what I always called you." She nearly drove off the road, she'd been so startled by her question. "And Mr. Randal, I know he's not going to be my teacher anymore, and that's really sad, but I want to call him Dad too. Do you think he'll care?"

"No, I don't think he would. You know that we're going to adopt you, correct?" She said that she did and was excited about that. "Your last name will be Calhoun, just like mine, and we'll be your parents. Just like Benson's parents."

"But they're going to let him keep his last name because his mom and dad were really super nice." She said that she'd heard that as well. "He'll be my cousin, and so will Aunt Noelle's babies too."

They talked about the babies on the way to the luncheon, and decided that Heather would like seventy sisters but no brothers. The two of them were still laughing as they entered the nice restaurant and were seated. Laney thought she could get used to this, just hanging out with people that knew how to have fun.

~~~

Rosemarie wasn't sure what was going on. Yes, she was in jail, but for what, she had no idea. The kid, she supposed, but that wasn't that big of a deal. She'd just wanted to spend some time with her granddaughter. Or daughter. However they flew it, that was fine by her.

"Hey, you. When am I gonna get out of here? You do know that you got nothing on me but seeing that kid." The officer said nothing as she passed around the trays with food on them. "Are you deaf? I asked you a question. I want to go and see my husband. He's in the hospital, you know."

"Mr. Price is going to be released today. And when he is, he's been told not to come and see you. Here is your lunch." She thought about tossing it back in her face, but she didn't look like she'd let her get by with it. "You want it or not? It's still six hours before dinner."

"I'll take it. It's crap, just so you know." But it hadn't been for breakfast, so she didn't figure this would be either. "I'll choke it down, I guess."

The bowl of vegetable soup was still steaming hot. And in addition to crackers, there was a thick ham sandwich with mayo on the side. Lettuce and tomato for it were in a large bowl, as well as a plate with cake on it for dessert. Carrot cake, her favorite. To drink she had tea and two cartons of milk, as well as a bottle of water. She hadn't eaten this well in ages.

When she was finished eating, Rosemarie looked around her cell. For the life of her, she could never get over how sparse they were. It was as if they wanted the criminals to be meaner when their time came to be let go. Nothing to show that they were only here for a little bit. Not even a clock or a calendar to mark off the days. She shook her head. They were gonna be real sorry when she was released.

"Ms. Pritchard?" She sat up and looked at the man in front of her cell. "I'm here on behalf of the court systems. You have indicated that you'd like to have legal representation with the state."

"I did?" He handed her a sheet of paper that looked like she'd scratched her name on it. "I don't even know what they're holding me for. I was just wanting to visit with my child."

She was going to leave it up to him on what he called the kid. It was her daughter, yeah, but maybe they all didn't know that. But then, Laney would have told them everything, just so she could keep her away from her dad.

"You took her without permission from her guardians, from their yard. In the process of committing this crime, you hurt her badly enough that she had to have stitches, as well as took her through an area that had been cordoned off by the police. That's not visiting, Ms. Prichard…that's kidnapping with intent to murder." She just waved him off. "I'm here to assure you that I'm going to do everything in my power to get you a reduced sentence for this crime. However—"

"Reduced? I think I should be just let go about that. I told you, I just wanted to visit her and my stepdaughter, Laney something…I didn't catch her last name now, she wasn't allowing it." The man said nothing. "Who the fuck are you anyway? Shouldn't you have me in some kind of nice room where there might be something for me to drink? This isn't the way that we should be talking about how you're getting me out of here."

"I apologize. My name is Chester, Phillip Chester. I work for Miller and Miller Law Firm." She asked him who had hired him. "No one. I'm doing this as pro bono, meaning that there won't be a charge for you."

"I know what that means, moron. Who got you to come here?" He said that he'd been commissioned by the state. "For taking my kid someplace?"

"From what I'm to understand, there are several more charges being levied against you. Not only kidnapping and attempted murder, but there is also a handful of robbery charges. Then there are some charges stemming from your own state of Florida concerning the kidnapping and trafficking of children." She asked him where he'd heard that, and waited while he pulled out a thick assed file. "Christ, is that all the people you have to see today?"

"No, this is your file. Florida was kind enough to send us what they had on you as well. Let me see here. Yes, you and an unnamed male went to the child clinic and took several children with the intent to sell them for profit. There are two witnesses to the kidnapping, as well as enough evidence to convict you."

"That unnamed male is Lance Price. My then live in

boyfriend." He asked her who her husband was. "I don't remember his name."

"It was Donald Prichard. He died some time ago under suspicious circumstances as well." She asked him where he was getting all this. "It's in your file. You should also be aware that if they find any of the children have been harmed or killed, they'll convict you for murder in the first degree."

"I thought you was supposed to be helping me, not telling me that I'm going to prison. What will it take for you to get me out of here with nothing more than a smack around or two? I know, I can tell you all about the unnamed male, Lance. He was the one that did all the planning and shit. If I tell you what he did, then I can get out, right?" He was shaking his head even before she finished. "Why the hell not?"

"Because he beat you to it." The lawyer might have still been talking, but all she could think about was that Lance had done her dirty. And not only that, but he was going to be getting off for shit they'd done together. That just wasn't right in her books. "Are you listening to me, Ms. Prichard? I asked you how you wanted to plea."

"I didn't do nothing that he didn't plan out and help me with. I mean, he made me go along with him on these things." He told her that that boat had sailed. Not like that, but that's what he meant. "I don't want you to tell me that. I want you to tell me how I get him into trouble instead of me."

"As I said, that's not going to happen now. He's given his testimony, and that's all there is to it. Now, as for your case, what would you like to plead on all the charges against you?"

"Not guilty." He asked her to be reasonable. "I am. If he can get off by telling lies about me, then I should be able to get out of here for the shit that he's done. And you know as well as I that ain't the least bit fair."

"All right. Not guilty. I'm assuming that you mean to have that as your plea on all the other charges as well." She said that she was fine by that. "You have a court appearance in the morning. Something will be brought for you to wear there. I'm afraid that it won't be anything that you brought with you, as the hotel took that for nonpayment. You'll need to settle up with them when you've been…when this is done."

"Good. When I'm out, then we'll talk about that." He told her not to make that many plans ahead of time. "You'll get me out of here. I have faith in you. I'm going to make all kinds of plans, because I know that I'm not going to prison for shit that he made me do."

None of it was true. She had planned and executed everything. Even going to so far as to go on a couple of things by herself so that she didn't have to share in the bounty. But it hadn't been like this before coming here. They'd been good partners in everything.

"This is all her fault." Rosemarie thought maybe blaming Laney with the death of her daughter was pushing it a little. She hadn't sent her any money to buy the drugs. Hell, she'd not even sent money when she had a birthday or Christmas. Laney was selfish, and she didn't have any heart.

The attorney arranged for her to go to a little room to talk. It wasn't what she wanted. They chained her to the table like she was a dog or something. When he laid out the things that she was in trouble for, she wondered how he was going to get her out. There sure was a lot of shit in his files, and she had to admit, it was a little scary.

As he prattled on about how she was going to be taken to court and that she wasn't to engage in conversation before, during, or after the hearing, she thought about Lance. The fucker was going to have to own up to his part in her plans. Or better yet, she wanted him to take the heat. Rosemarie couldn't be in prison. She was too much of a social person, and she didn't do social in jail. Fuckity fuck fuck.

CHAPTER 10

Standing in the shower, Randal heard the door open and close and smiled. Laney had said she was going to join him, but as the time grew later, he wasn't so sure he'd have time. School was back in session today, and he had to get there early.

"I'm sorry." He turned and pulled her into his arms just as she reached for him. "There was a problem with a backpack that had to be addressed. And then shoes were missing too."

"Having a child in the house means I'm going to have to seduce you whenever I can." He kissed her, giving her as much of his passion as he could. "Christ, I need you."

He pressed her against the shower stall wall and devoured her mouth. Then moving down her body, he nibbled on her throat that was pounding with her pulse. Her breasts were suckled on as he made his way down to her navel, his favorite place to tickle her when she was naked.

"You have to hurry, Randal. All I thought about all the time I was looking for a shoe was coming in here and having you make me come." He grinned at her from his position on the floor. "You're going to pay for making me wait."

"I hope so." He spread her nether lips and suckled on her clit. She was soaking wet now, not just with the shower water, but she was dripping wet too. As he made a meal out of her, savoring every drop of her, he slid his finger into her heat and told her to come.

She cried out with her release, quietly because they didn't want Heather to hear her. They'd had a close call two days ago when they'd thought that she was at a friend's house, but she'd come back early because the child had gotten sick.

Standing up, he told Laney that he loved her and then kissed her again as he slid deep inside of her. She was so tight around him, and when she came, tightening around him again and again, Randal moaned at the ecstasy of her.

"My turn." He hadn't come yet but it didn't matter. When she pushed him back against the wall, he knew that he'd come sooner or later. And from the look on her face, he had a feeling it was going to be later. She cupped his balls in her hands and rolled them. Randal's eyes rolled to the back of his head and he nearly fell forward.

She never touched her mouth to him, not yet anyway. But she did make him suffer, in ways that he was sure were harder on him than being hurt. Christ, he loved this woman, and when she finally took him into her luscious mouth, he cried out loudly as he came hard enough to make his body ache with it. When she swallowed him, taking his crown past the tightness of her throat, he came a second time. His body bowed back from the wall; his entire being seemed to have clenched up seconds before his release. As soon as his cock and balls emptied, he slid to the floor, his legs no longer strong enough to support his weight.

"You killed me." Her giggle had him looking at her, but even his vision was protesting the movement. "I cannot move. And all the kids in my class are going to be so disappointed."

"You think so? Well, if you're a good boy today, I'll make is worth your while when you get back." He groaned. "Poor baby. Do you want me to kiss it and make it better?"

"No. Don't touch me. You really will kill me." The water shut off and he still couldn't move. "Call me off sick, I beg you. I can't move."

"Heather needs a ride to school, and I have a meeting to go to. Get up and show some spirit." Randal did stand up, but he was wobbly because his legs felt like rubber. "You owe me, if I made you feel this good."

"As I said, I think you killed me. Or broke me...I'm not sure."

She was laughing when she left the bedroom. He dressed himself with the magic and made his way to the stairs. Standing there, he heard Heather talking to Laney downstairs in the hallway and waited.

"Is it going to be scary, you think?" Laney told her that Randal would never allow harm to come to either of them. "I know, but I don't know if I can do it. Are you sure that he won't hurt me?"

"As positive as I have been about anything in my life." Randal didn't know who they were talking about, but he'd bet anything that it was their dad. "I'll be right there with you, as will Randal. You don't have to worry about anything, of this I swear to you."

Lance had requested to see Heather. He told them that he'd not do anything to hurt her, nor would he touch her unless she said it was all right. Lance had taken on many changes in the last few days. Walking the neighborhood that he now lived in. Going to work every day, even on his days off, to help out, and he wasn't begging Laney for anything. Other than to see Heather.

"I'd like to tell her that I'm sorry too." Laney had said nothing, but Randal asked him what it was that he'd done that he needed to tell her that. "I wasn't there for her either. I was a lousy father to both my daughters. One was completely my fault. The other, Heather, I could have said something. Even though I'm pretty sure she's not my daughter, I was around when she was born and I should have stood up for her. Done something that would have made her life better."

"She lived with monsters; you know that, don't you?" He nodded at Laney when she spoke. "They were drug addicts, and treated her like a slave. She had to cook and clean for them, and keep them out of harm's way when they were too stoned to take care of her. You did that to her. You and Rosemarie."

"I know that. I should have...I should have done a lot of things that I didn't. And every day for the rest of my life, I will beg for forgiveness and peace for what I've done. Not that I deserve either, but I know that I was wrong about so many things." Laney didn't say anything, so Lance looked at Randal. "I only want to tell her how sorry I am. To beg her to please try and forgive me. If you both wish to be there, then that's all right with me as well. I don't deserve to be alone with anyone, as far as I'm concerned."

And today, she was going to go and talk to him. Randal had agreed to take her, as Laney wasn't sure she could handle it. Of late she'd been very teary and upset. He hoped that once the trial was over for Rosemarie, things for her would settle

148

down.

By the time they two of them were at the school, he'd talked Heather into joining the after school singing club, as well as trying out for track. She loved to be active, and he was sure that she'd enjoy some sort of sports too. As soon as she was out of the car and on her way into the building, he picked up his things and made his way to the building as well. But once he was on the sidewalk, he had an eerie feeling that something was wrong.

There were no children hanging around the play yard. The buses didn't show up for another hour at least, so he was sure that was it. But the feeling wouldn't be quelled, so he called Heather back and she came immediately.

"I want you to go to the car and wait for me." She nodded, but grabbed his hand. "I don't know what's going on, honey, but I can feel it."

"I can too. Like there is someone inside there that is hurting." He only felt apprehensive about something, not sure what it was. But when she said hurting, he lifted his nose to the air and could smell it then. Blood. "Dad, I want to go home."

"I can't leave here without knowing." She nodded and tightened her grip on his hand. "Go to the car and stay there. I'm going to have my brothers come here as well."

She made her way to the car by back stepping. She was nervous, he knew that, but at what, he didn't know. His own heart was pounding, and he knew that he was going to walk into a shit storm. Taking a deep breath, he let it out slowly as he reached out to the family for help.

Joe and I are in town. I'm on my way. Joe said not to enter. She doesn't know what is going on, but don't go inside. He said that

149

he couldn't do that. *Yeah, I told her that you would do it anyway. Just be careful, Randal. I don't want to have to explain to Mom or your mate that you were hurt.*

The first thing he saw was a trail of blood. Not a great deal of it, but enough to let him know that someone was inside the place. He told Trent and the others what he found, and they assured him that they were coming. That was when he saw the police officer who dropped his little boy off every morning.

He's dead. Shot once in the head. I have his gun. Chloe asked him where Heather was. *In my car. I told her not to move until one of you guys or I came back to get her. Can someone tell Laney? I need to be on my.... Mrs. Collins is dead. Her body is just behind the front desk. I don't think that was where she was killed. There is no splatter.*

His brothers started talking all at once. He had to close the connection for a few moments just to get his breath back. The smell of blood was making his wolf crazy. The need to protect and kill was making him a little high strung.

Randal felt rather than heard Laney. She was upset, but when she spoke to him, he could feel her trying hard to control her terror. He was glad for it...he was afraid enough as it was.

While I understand that you have to check the place out, you get hurt and I will hunt you down and hurt you worse. Randal told her that he loved her. *I love you too. Please be careful. I'm not going to tell you to get out of there...I understand why you need this. But please, for me, stay safe.*

I promise you that I will. He stepped over the body of a child, and his heart tore up when he realized it was one of his kids. *I can't talk to you now, love. I have to finish this. Please, just let me.*

Yes, I understand.

He didn't tell her what he'd seen, didn't tell any of them what he came across as he made his way to his classroom. Randal had no idea why, but he thought this had nothing to do with him, but the school itself.

As soon as he stepped into his room, he saw three of his students huddled in the corner. It took him several minutes to get them out of the room through the windows. Trent was there, lifting them over the glass and to the ground and safety. When they were out and running toward the rest of his family, both Chloe and Marty joined him in the room. Trent was going to wait there for more children. Anastasia joined them as they headed down the hall again.

"There are children in the gym. The gunman, or gunmen, are not in there. I'm going to lead them to this room, then to Trent." He nodded at Anastasia. "I don't know the people that did this, but you can bet that they're not long for this world when I find them."

She went to the gym and left the door ajar. When it closed all the way, he had a moment of panic until he heard from Trent. He told him that he was outside the gym door helping the children there to safety. Randal had to lean against the wall and get his terrified heart back under control.

At the fork in the hallway they decided that they needed to split up. They'd cover more ground that way, and maybe find more children. Chloe took the right fork and Marty the other. Randal made his way to the cafeteria, where he knew that the kids gathered before classes began.

As soon as he entered the great room, he thought that the children there were dead. They were lined up on the floor, their heads down and their little bodies as still as he'd ever seen them. There were perhaps fifty students in the room, and two adults. He was sure that one of them was a teacher, but he'd not seen her face yet. The other, he had no idea. As soon as Mrs. Cavendish turned in his direction, he felt his world tumble around him. The new principal was not only holding a gun in her hands, but she had blood all over her face and dress.

She hadn't seen him as yet, for which he was grateful. But he had to get to the children, or at least get them to safety. He told the others what he found, and when Chloe told him that she had a group of children she was taking to the gym, Marty said she was on her way to him.

No, don't come here. I can handle this. She asked him why not. *Because if you come here with me, I'm going to do everything in my power to protect you, even at my own risk. I love you for your help, but I can't concentrate on what I'm doing if you are here, and I'll get hurt. Please, let me do this on my own. If I can't, I'll call you. But for now, I have this.*

All right, but like your mate, if you get hurt, I'm going to hurt you worse. He said he would let them, too. *I'm with Chloe, looking for other children. If they're the only two, then we can work quicker to get the strays out. These poor children and their parents.*

He had to agree. But he had to somehow end this without anyone dying. He wasn't sure what he could do, if he was honest with himself, but he had to do it quickly. Almost as soon as he thought he should call in help, Mrs. Cavendish— her first name escaped him right now—picked up one of the students by the hair and put the gun to his head.

"Don't." Randal moved out of the doorway he'd been hiding in and moved toward her. "I'm not armed."

He'd slipped the gun in the back of his pants before coming

out. And when no one searched him, he was profoundly glad. The gun might be the difference between the life and death of these children.

"Well, look who it is. Mr. Randal. You come to die too?" He glanced at the other man, but didn't speak. "I've had enough of these little shits, and I've come here today to rid the world of their whiney voices."

"You don't want to do that. Laura, right? Your first name is Laura." Randal smiled when she nodded. "I'm terrible with names. I think it has to do with having to remember so many. What are you doing here?"

"Killing the scum of the earth. What are you doing here?" He told her he was coming to work. "Well, you should have called off, I think. Every one of these little pissers is going to die today. My name will go down in history around these parts as the woman who did the world a favor by killing a bunch of kids."

"And your help? Who is that?" He thought it was her husband, but he wasn't sure. Randal had met the man once, when she was named the new principal of the school. "You think you need help with a bunch of children?"

"My husband and I, we're ready to die for our cause. I didn't think I had one until these little shits kept coming by my office and begging me for shit. I don't have time for that. I'm supposed to be retired, not working all the time here." He wasn't sure what she was talking about, but she continued before he could ask. "Harold lost his job a week ago. Right before Christmas. Can you believe that shit? That man—your friend, Doug Coulier—fired him because he was drinking on the job. My husband does not have a problem with drinking. If anything, he should be drinking more with the shit that he's gone through."

"What is it he's going through, Laura?" She fired the gun at his feet and he didn't move. The children, however, started to scream. Laura shot one of them at random and told them to shut the fuck up. "Laura, why don't you let them go? They're not going to be any help to you in this."

"He and I are going to make some demands, then we're going to go away for a long time." Laura smiled at her husband. "Aren't we baby? We're going to take a long vacation."

When she lifted her gun up and pointed it at him, Randal thought for sure he was going to break his promise to Laney. But when she fired at her husband, just a single shot, the man fell backward, hitting the wall behind him before he fell on the floor. Randal was terrified.

"He lost his job and all our money. Now I'm going to go to prison, and I don't think I can handle that, Randal. What am I doing here?" He said he didn't know. "I don't either. I hurt all up in my head. They all have to die, you know. But you have to as well."

The gun was lifted up and pointed it at him, and he did the only thing he could think of. Randal drew his own gun and fired three times, his hand jerking with each shot. When she fell backwards and then lay still, Randal sat down. He had just killed someone.

~~~

Tanner waited with the rest of his family for Randal to be processed. His clothing, as well as his shoes, had to be removed, and he was then checked again. Even though he'd told them several times that he'd not been hurt, they looked him over for wounds. None of them, not even Laney, who had arrived just as the police were entering the building, could touch him yet.

"I think she was mad at her husband." The officer asked him again if he'd heard his name. "No, I'm sorry. I only just remembered her name when she turned toward me. I think she's only been employed for a few weeks. Right after Thanksgiving she was named as principal."

"Did you know any of the students?" Randal told him that he knew all the kids in the school. "I'm sorry, sir. I truly am. We're still going through the building now, but it looks like you and the chief got most of them out before this went down."

Randal looked at Laney and him when he said his name. "I'm all right. I promise. Shook up a lot, but I'm okay." Laney told him that she loved him. "And I you, sweetheart. You were all I could think of when she pointed the gun at me."

Tanner bent down to his brother's level and asked him what he needed from him. "The principal's home is going to be gone through. Also the computer in her office. They'll want to take you to the hospital, just to make sure that you're not in shock, so let them. Better to have a record of this than not."

"I understand." Laney asked if she could hold Randal's hand, and the cop nodded but warned her not to touch him anywhere else just yet. "I'm all right."

He kept saying that, and Tanner had a feeling that he was trying to convince himself as much as them. His parents weren't able to come into the building just yet, nor was anyone else for that matter. Tanner had only been allowed in because his brother had asked for a lawyer and his wife. The rest of them would have to wait. But Tanner was giving them updates about what was going on.

The parents of the kids had started coming to the school

about ten minutes after it hit the news. There were going to be a lot of grief stricken families tonight. Four children had been murdered, two of them from the upper classes; sixth grade, he'd heard. Also one of Randal's kids, as well as a young girl who had wanted to escort her little brother in today. Then there was the police officer, as well as the secretary to the principal. It would be a long time before motive was sorted out, but Tanner would be there for his family.

When Randal was released, Tanner stayed back to let the rest of them hug him. Randal had saved the lives of a great many children today, and quite a few adults. Mrs. Cavendish had been waiting on the rest of the staff to come in, and her plan, according to the list she had on her desk when searched, was that she was going to kill each teacher as they came in. Then when the children were in their rooms, she was going to have them line up against the walls and kill them as well. It would have been a massacre of the highest kind. As it was, there were still too many deaths as far as they were concerned.

Tanner waited until the last of the bodies was brought out. The principal and her spouse were taken out the back of the building and not with the others. He thought it was a good idea, as the crowd was already gearing up for a showdown. As he watched them cling together, their hearts broken as much as his was, he wondered what would happen now. This school was jinxed as far as he was concerned.

"They're going to rebuild it." He looked at Noah when he spoke from the dark shadows of the building next door. "I've put the word out that it needs to be torn down and began anew. I'm going to pay for it."

"We'll help too." Noah thanked him. "They're going to need to find teachers that will come here too. And a new principal."

"I think your brother would make a good one. Look how he's calming down everyone, telling them that the people are no longer going to hurt their children. Telling them not what they want to hear, but what he knows for facts. He's a good man, and will be good for the new school. A man with a family. A heart made for children. He needs to take this job so that it'll be run well, and more security can come in and make it safe. He'll be able to do that." Tanner told him that Randal had turned it down before. "I don't think he'll be able to this time. To them, he's a hero — me as well — and if he doesn't take it, they'll come to him anyway with any problems."

"He's going to fall apart when this is done." Noah said that he would, but he'd have his family there. "Yes, we'll be there for him. So will his mate."

"I'm to understand that you're not looking for your mate. That you'd rather spend your days alone than with her." Tanner turned to look at the vampire, and asked him where he'd heard that. "I'm not a man who tells on those that come to me."

"Yes, I don't...I didn't want a mate. But I can see now where one would be good for a person. Look at Laney and how she's there for him, but not in his way." Noah said he doubted that she would be thought of as being in the way. "No, I guess not. But while she's there for him, she's giving him the time to come to terms with it too. Do you know what I mean?"

"Yes. They're a good team. Just as your own mate will be with you." Tanner said nothing. He wasn't sure about that. He was sort of set in his ways, even for as young as he was. "Tanner, she will love you like no other, and you will her as well. But to turn one away, a love like no other, simply because you think yourself above it all, would be a disaster for you both."

"I know that. I do." He looked back at the man who had been his friend for only a few weeks and told him the truth, the truth that he'd not been able to tell anyone before. "When I was in college, there was a car accident. Two people were hurt, me being one of them. I can't father children. Not ever."

"I know that. I think they all do." He looked back at his family and asked Noah how they might know. "I would imagine that Joe has told Trent. She would have done a great deal of research on your family before coming to you the first time. It would have been easy enough for her to find and dig into."

"I should have known that it would be out there. The way my mom and grandda treated me when I got home that summer. Joe, she told you then?" He said that she told him everything about his family. "There's more?"

"Oh yes, a great deal more. Some of it you might already be aware of, some you might not. She is good at research. Benny is good too, but not as good as my Joe is." Tanner nodded but said nothing. "Do you think that your family will love you less because you cannot father children?"

"No, it's not that. Just that they might...I don't know. I guess I don't want to disappoint anyone. I know that I am. When I woke up in the hospital with my nuts banged up, it was too late for me to shift and take care of the damage. Besides, the bruising was so bad that it wouldn't have helped me much anyway. I was hurt too badly." Noah said nothing, for which he was grateful. "What if she wants a passel of children, as my grandda says? What if her only desire is to have my child? I can't do that, for anyone."

"I think that when the right woman comes along, she will be so happy to have a man like you in her life that she will be only too happy to just be with you." Tanner looked at Noah with a cocked brow. "Yes, it sounded better in my head than past my lips. But you'll be fine, young Tanner. You and your family are meant to have it all, and she will give it to you. You and your family will be complete then."

"Sure, so long as no one asks me about a baby to bounce on their knee."

The police officer that had been first on the scene came toward him. Glancing back at Noah, he wasn't surprised to see that he had disappeared. It wasn't late in the day, but the police weren't as accepting of vampires as they were wolves.

"Mr. Calhoun, there is a call for you from the station. It's about that woman, Ms. Prichard. She wants to talk to the attorney for her daughter. I'm assuming that would be you?" He said it was. "She's an ornery person, if you ask me. I don't know how she got along this long without someone hitting her a few times to keep her in line."

"I don't either. I'll go, but I'll have an officer with me." He said that was a good idea. "Her attorney, Chester, has he been notified?"

"Yes, sir, he has been. But she said she doesn't want to talk to him. She called him some names, but he'll be there directly." Tanner thanked him. "You're welcome. I'll be glad when she moves on. Like I said, she's mean."

CHAPTER 11

Phillip sat on the bench and waited for Tanner. Tanner was a good attorney, and a better man than he'd ever worked with. Not that they were working together on this, but Phillip wanted to be like him and liked by him. As he sat there thinking of all the crap that Rosemarie had been telling him, all he could think about was getting out on his own and becoming an attorney that he liked. Not this flunky that had to take the pro bono cases that no one else wanted. When he saw Tanner pull up in front of the station, he stood up.

"She doesn't want me to be in there with you, and threw a fit when they told her I had to be." Tanner said that they could both go to the bar and have some lunch until it was okay to have a beer. "Yes, I'd like that as well. She's a pain in the butt."

"Yes, she is. But whatever she wants, I'm recording it." Phillip hadn't brought his own recorder, but knew that he should be recording this conversation too, as they were supposed to be on opposite sides of this case. Phillip had pulled his out of his briefcase at his desk at work and had

161

forgotten to put it back. "I'll send you a copy of whatever it has on it. She just might want to plea down or something."

The two of them entered the room. Phillip had asked for the room to be recorded, both with video and sound. He wasn't taking any chances with this woman saying that anyone hadn't given her a fair shake. As soon as he sat down with Tanner at his side, she told him to go away, she wanted to talk to Tanner.

"He's not going anywhere, Rosemarie. He is representing you in this case that is being put before a judge in the morning. You called for this meeting, now tell me what you want so I can go home." She told him that she wanted to see Lance, alone, and without chains. "No. Anything else?"

"I don't like you very much. He's my husband and I want to talk to him. I know that you can't let him take the stand against me because we're married." Tanner said that they weren't, and he asked her for a copy of the license if she had one. "I don't have it on me. They took all my shit when they brought me here. But we're married, you check it out."

"We have. You're not married. You were at one time to someone else—who we're having exhumed, by the way—but you were never wed to Lance Price." Tanner was cool and calm, and Phillip tried to emulate him. "If that is all you wanted from me, you could have asked your own attorney who would have contacted me. I have nothing more to say to you."

Phillip stood up when Tanner did. Rosemarie tried to stand as well, but the chains at her wrists and legs were hampering her. She told them both to sit, she wasn't done, and neither of them did. Whatever she wanted, she wasn't going to get it from Tanner.

"I want whatever you gave Lance." Phillip asked her what she meant. "You shut your pie hole, you idiot, I'm talking to him. He got himself a good bargain, I'm betting. Lance did, didn't he? Well I have shit on him too."

"No you don't. And if you talk to him like that again, I'll get you for threatening someone." She sneered at him. "I mean it, Rosemarie, I won't put up with this. I have better things to do than sit here and listen to your drivel. You have a hearing in the morning, and I'll see you then."

"I don't deserve to go to jail. I did nothing wrong but want to see my granddaughter."

When she started sobbing Phillip started to reach for her, he had no idea why, but as soon as Tanner pushed him back away from her, he saw the pen sticking out of his arm. She'd stabbed him with it.

"Just sit down." He said that he was sitting. "No, you're standing on wobbly feet. Just slide to the floor for me while the officer takes her back to her cell."

"All right." He wasn't sure what she might have done had he been in here alone with her. Or to Tanner. But she had tried to kill him. At least that's what he thought.

"She did." He asked Tanner what he meant. "You're talking out loud. You wondered if she tried to kill you or me, and you said it aloud. The ambulance is coming. Once it gets here, I'll call your firm and let them know what she did."

"I need to come and work for you." He said that he didn't have a practice except his family and a friend of his. "I can help you. Even if it's only to do research on cases. I can't go back to that firm. And they'll probably fire me after this anyway. I'm on the shit list. Every nasty job that comes in, they put it on my desk."

He looked at the pen sticking out of his forearm. It made him slightly sick to see it there, with the blood dripping down to his elbow. Laying his head on his other arm while Tanner held his injured one, he tried to think where she had gotten the pen. The woman that was standing near him when he looked up smiled at him.

"The Feds sent you in?" She said that she had come on her own, and told him what her name was. "Hello, Anastasia Coulier. I'm an idiot."

"The pen isn't yours, but that of an officer that works here. He left it for her to write a list of things she wanted in the way of food. He'll be reprimanded. You, however, aren't going to be fired. If they try, I'll come there and make them see reason." He asked her if she was going to kill them. "Not unless it comes to that."

When she laughed, he wasn't so sure she wasn't serious. She looked it. In fact, he thought she looked like she could kill them all without much in the way of effort. When the medical team entered the small room, he asked Tanner to stay with him, he wanted some company.

He was taken to the hospital where they were going to remove the pen. It was evidence, and they were afraid that someone would touch it and hurt him more. Phillip wasn't sure that he could be hurting any less. The pain was starting to make itself known to him in a big way.

"I have a sister...she's not going to be happy with me if she hears about this on the news. It will be on there, right?" Tanner told him he'd call her. "Yes, her name is Bridget McGowan. Her husband, Rogan McGowan, is a bastard, so if he answers, just hang up. He won't give her the message anyway."

"If it helps you at all, I'll have an officer go there and get her for you." Phillip told him that would only be worse on her. "I see. Is she in an abusive relationship then?"

"You have no idea. She's left him several times. And while she's still with him, it's not like you think. She goes back when he threatens the kids. She has four of them. Well, he has four. She doesn't have any, thankfully, but when she leaves, he hurts the kids. And they're all she has, she told me."

"I'll see to her." Phillip thanked him as they inserted an IV in his other arm and gave him something for pain. "You just let the meds kick in."

"Christ love a doodle. That's nice." He was floating. And every time he tried to open his mouth to tell Tanner again where she was and to be careful, he felt himself sliding down a slippery slope of drugs that he couldn't fight. When Tanner asked him for Bridget's address again, he pointed to his phone, telling him it was in that. Phillip let the drugs take him under then. He could no longer fight them.

When he woke the next time, his arm was in a sling above his head, his body was heavy, like he'd been encased in concrete, and his mouth was dry. Looking around the room, he saw that he had visitors, but couldn't make out who they were. When she spoke, he smiled.

"You could have been killed, then where would I be?" Phillip told her that she was his benefactor with his insurance. "If that's supposed to be funny, I'm not laughing. What happened?"

"I did something incredibly stupid and paid the price. Are you here alone?" He tried to look around, but his head was very heavy too. "I'm so thirsty. Can you get me something?"

"The doctor said you could only have ice shavings." He

looked at Tanner and thanked him for bringing his sister. "It was my pleasure. She is going to be staying here tonight. Her husband is in jail. He tried to stop us from leaving."

When he didn't say anything, Phillip thought about asking if he'd been hurt. But the man was huge, and while Rogan was big too, his was mostly due to eating fatty foods and drinking. It mattered little to him what kind of booze it was, so long as it was cheap and he could drink all he wanted without being bothered.

"I'm hoping that he stays there too. At least long enough for me to get some distance this time. And the kids are relieved as well." He looked at Tanner when he shook his head slightly. "We don't have a lot of funds, but Mr. Calhoun here, he's offered to help us out. Even set us up with a nice place in Las Vegas that we can stay in until we get up on our feet."

"We?" She nodded at him and told him he was coming too. "Honey, I can't leave here. I have commitments and a job. Leaving here would.... I can't even practice law out there. I don't have a license."

Tanner cleared his throat before speaking. "That's been arranged too. I have a couple of friends that are making it so you can take the bar exam there and be fully licensed. Also, the place that we have set up for the six of you will be rent free for one year. More if you need it." Phillip thought this was too much, not to mention going too fast. "Her husband will only be in jail for forty-eight hours, Phillip. And you know as well as I do that once he's free, he's going to come after you when he can't find his wife and children."

Phillip thought about telling him that he could handle the man, but he couldn't. Rogan was a man who talked with his fists and not his mouth, unless it was to spew racial slurs and comments that were crude. Instead, he thanked Tanner.

"My family is the one to thank. They have a fund set up for just this sort of occurrences. And it does happen a great deal. All the arrangements are made. All you guys need to do is pack what you need at your homes, and someone will pick you up and take you to the airport. One of my brothers will go with you to show you around the area and make sure you have all that you need." He thanked Tanner again. So did Bridge. "We want to help you. And also, your firm has been notified here. It's all taken care of."

In less time than he thought it should have taken, they were all packed, with the help of some very nice people, their things loaded onto a large jet, and they were on their way. Phillip was so overwhelmed that when one of his nephews came to sit on his lap, he was shocked by it.

"They were never allowed to touch Rogan very much. You know how he was about people." Phillip did know. "When we get settled, Phillip, I want you to be happy too. It's about time, don't you think?"

"I am happy, Bridge. I have been for a long time." She just shook her head. "And what about you? How happy are you?"

"I'm going to get a fresh start with my kids. I know that they're not of my body, but I love them as much as if they were. I won't leave them to him. And I have you close should I need you. I don't think I could be any happier than that. But you, you've gone without for a long time. And we both know why." He didn't comment. There were few people who knew anything about him and his sexual preferences. "I want you to find yourself someone and settle down. There won't be people there that will hurt you because of it."

167

"Rogan was the only one that did." She told him she was sorry. "Don't be. As I've told you before, I'm fine. Happy too now that you're going to be getting everything that you deserve."

He looked down at his arm and the sling that was wrapped around it. There was something there, an envelope. Pulling it out so that no one would see it, he opened it up and looked inside. There was a note with some cash. Heading to the bathroom, he read it and counted the money.

"Phillip, good luck with your future. The boards have been taken care of and you have an office set up. My brother, Sterl, he's going to show you where it is. Here is some cash to tide you over until you start working. And Sterl is going to use you for the business dealings he has there. Good luck, Tanner."

There was ten grand in the envelope, as well as a gift card for a pizza place that he'd never heard of. Phillip sat in the bathroom and sobbed. He just could not believe the kindness of this family. And he was going to make it right too, by being the best attorney that he could be.

~~~

Lance sat in the back of the courtroom. He wished he could sit up front with his daughters, but he wasn't going to push himself into their lives. It was hard enough even facing them after what he'd done. But this was better, and Laney had invited him over for dinner tonight. He was taking this one day at a time, and was happy with what she'd give him.

After the room was called to order, he watched the doors that would bring out Rosemarie. She had a lot going against her, and he was glad now that he'd been able to distance himself from her, even after all that he'd done too. When she was brought out, in a suit that wasn't her style, he felt himself shrink up a bit, not wanting her to see him. They chained her to the floor and desk, and he wondered about that.

They were listing off her charges when little Heather came back to sit with him. He put her on the chair next to him, but she climbed into his lap. It was the first time either of them had come to him first. And the first time since he'd sent Heather away that he'd held her. When she looked up at him, he simply fell in love with her.

"You're my dad." He said that he was. "I'm not going to call you Daddy. I want to call you Mr. Randal. Is that okay?"

"Yes, it's perfectly fine with me, so long as you know that I'm your father, it's fine with me." She nodded and looked up front. He wasn't sure what to say to her, so didn't say anything. Lance didn't know that many children, and wasn't sure how to interact with them anymore.

"That mean lady up there is my mom, huh?" He said that she was. And she was mean. "I don't like her at all. She tried to kill me. And she cut open my head like a melon."

He laughed. It was said with such venom that he wanted to hug her to him and laugh again. But the room turned to look at them, so he held her and told her she needed to keep it down.

The things that were brought against Rosemarie were long and harsh. There was a great deal of it that he'd participated in, and some that he'd had no idea. The part about stealing the children and selling them, he'd had no idea that was what she'd done. She had told him over and over that the children were going to families, not to some third world country to be sold as slaves and as sex partners. Lance had cried for two days when he'd heard that part.

"When am I going to get a deal?" Lance wasn't sure that she'd been offered one, so he listened to Rosemarie's questions. "I should get a deal too. It's all his fault, all this. I was just an innocent victim in Lance's schemes."

"You will not address this courtroom without permission. And that will come from me." Rosemarie waved the judge off. "You will keep your comments to yourself and wait until someone asks you a direct question. This is my courtroom and my rules."

"That work for you?" The judge looked at Rosemarie's attorney when she spoke again. "I'm not going to sit here and have you pass whatever it is you're thinking of doing without me getting a deal too. I didn't do shit."

"Ms. Prichard, I'm not warning you again. Keep your mouth shut." She stood up as best she could, and told him to make her. The courtroom was as quiet as he'd ever heard it. "Bailiff, take Ms. Prichard back to her cell, and we'll proceed with this case without her presence."

"You can't fucking do that. I have a right, just like everybody else, to have myself some good shit given to me too. I want you to cut me a deal. I don't want to spend not one day in prison. I didn't do shit." She was being dragged out, literally kicking and screaming at them all. "You mother fucker, you're going to pay for this shit. Where is Lance? He's the one that made me do all this. He needs to be brought here and made to get me out of this. It's his fault."

He started to stand. In fact, he set Heather on the seat next to him so that he could. But she grabbed his hand and shook her head. He told her that it was his name and he thought to calm her.

"She's weird. And mean. You stand up and she's gonna

hit you too. She might even split your melon so bad that you spill out your brain." He told her that he was sorry that she'd been hurt. "Me too, but you got no reason to be hurt too. I don't like her, but I do you. So far."

He'd take it. Even if she only liked him for the next hour, Lance would take it. So he remained in his seat and Heather climbed into his lap again. It was right then that he realized that not only had he been a fool, but that he could make a difference in his life. Starting today.

While he wasn't sure how he was going to make this work, he was going to do it. To have someone look up to him again, even so far as she'd said, was something that he'd missed. Lance hadn't been the best of fathers, especially after his wife had passed, but he was given a second chance here and he wasn't going to mess it up. Thinking about all the things he'd been up to and what he was doing now, he thought how lucky he was that either of his daughters would allow him to be in the same room with them. Lance had been a failure.

"You think too hard." He told Heather that he did at that. "You have to chill. That's what Dad tells me all the time when I can't get something to work. He said to stop thinking too hard and it'll come to you."

"Does it work?" She nodded at him with a huge grin. "Well, I think I can start thinking less hard if you come around sometimes and tell me that. I do get all messed up at times."

"Mom said it's because you had a bad fluid." He started to ask her what she meant by that when she shook her head. "No. Not fluid. That's like water. But I don't remember how to say it."

"Influence. I have had a bad influence." She told him that was it. "She's right. I did. But I'm not going to let that happen to me again."

Lance listened to the goings on in the courtroom. His mind was about half on it, the other on things he wanted to do. He had a nice place to stay now, but it lacked personal things. Which wasn't to say he had any to add there, but he was going to make some. Pictures. He needed to add some pictures to his walls. Then he remembered that all this things from his house had been put in storage. Things that he was going to get out and see if Laney would want any. There was a great deal of it too.

As soon as the courtroom proceedings broke for lunch, he made his way to Laney and her husband carefully. He was never sure about being welcome. Not that she did anything to make him feel that way, but he supposed it was his own thoughts and feelings. Heather asked if they could go and get pizza together, and when Randal told her sure, Lance started to step away.

"You'll join us, won't you, Dad?" Lance nearly wept, he was so happy that Laney would include him, but only nodded. "Good. I wanted to talk to you about a job that we might have for you. I know that at one time you used to coach my baseball team, and there is a need for some coaches."

"It's been a long time, honey. I don't know if I remember all the rules." She told him, as they made their way out of the big building, that they had courses for coaches, even teaching them how to keep score and some CPR classes. "I'd like that. I work only part time now, but I can see the schedule for it and help out. I'd like that."

"I'm going to play too. I never been on a baseball team before." He thought about teaching his little girl baseball and smiled. "I got me a bat for Christmas, but I'm not allowed to hit nobody with it, and I can't break any windows or Mr. Wally said I have to do hard labor. He already makes me take the trash out to learn how to earn my keep. He's a good cooker, so I don't want him mad at me."

They were still laughing about it as they made their way into the restaurant. Lance thought about the storage units he had and mentioned it to Laney. The look on her face made him think that she was upset with him, but when she thanked him, over and over, he asked her what she was feeling.

"I don't know. I thought, I guess you can understand why, but I thought that you'd sold it all off when you left with Rosemarie." He said that she'd tried to talk him into it, but he'd not been such a bad person then. "I don't think you were bad, not really, Dad…just misguided. And yes, I'd love to have some of the things from the house. What are you going to do with it? I mean, I thought that had been sold too."

"No. Even if I had wanted to, I couldn't have. It has belonged to you since your momma passed." She said that she didn't know that. "I didn't either until about a week or so after the funeral. I had just met Rosemarie, I think, so I might not have gotten around to telling you. I messed up on that."

"No, you did the right thing, I think. Had she known, there is no telling what she might have done to make me turn it over to the two of you." He was glad that she was eager not to blame him solely on this, but he might well have done it too.

The rest of the lunch was spent talking about the upcoming spring festival at the school. Not only did Lance volunteer to help out, but he got talked into baking cookies to sell at the bake sale. All in all, he thought it was the best meal he'd ever had.

CHAPTER 12

Rogan was pissed off. His wife was gone, and her pisser of a brother was missing too. And his house had been fucked with. Wherever she was, Bridget was gonna pay, and pay big time. As he wandered through the house, trying his best to make a counting of all the shit that was missing, he was also mad because he couldn't even make a report about it. He, first of all, wasn't supposed to be near this place, and secondly, if she took it then it was hers to do with what she wanted. Fucking bitch.

He came out of their bedroom, after shitting on the bed, to find a man standing in his living room. Since he'd never seen him before Rogan puffed out his chest, and was sorely disappointed that his belly was still hanging out there more.

"What the hell do you want? You got a lot of nerve coming into a man's house unannounced." He said that he had called out. "I was busy."

"Yes, so I can smell. You actually shit on a bed that you may well have to sleep in? Whatever. I've come to tell you that Bridget and your children are no longer living here. Nor is her brother, Phillip. They have moved on, and I would suggest that you do something about it." The man looked around the place, and for some reason Rogan was even more pissed off that he seemed to find it lacking. "You might want to find yourself a job, as well as some sort of residence other than this one. The reason I say that is, when the state finds out that you are no longer living here with your family, they'll have you move on soon. This is a place for families that are too lazy to find good work, not a man bent on making others suffer."

"Who the hell are you, coming in here, telling me what you think I want to know about? I can damn well see that she's not here and that she's taken my kids. There's laws about that. See if I don't call me someone in to sue her too." He just smiled, and that was when he saw his fangs. "You thinking of killing me, vamp? I got news for you, I ain't going to be easy for you."

Rogan found himself a foot or so off the floor, and the man was holding him there with just his one hand. Rogan didn't struggle, even if he could have. The vamp would kill him and he'd never get his family back.

"Now, I should like to start over, this time with your undivided attention. I cannot kill you, yet, but I will should you force my hand. And since I know that you will, sooner or later, I suggest that you get your things in order so that your family members will benefit from your slow and painful death. Blink once if you can understand me." He did, slowly, so that he'd know that he was listening. "Now. I know that you have a brother and a sister. Both are attorneys from what I'm to understand. Blink again."

He did as he was told and was let down. The man leaned back against the wall while Rogan tried to get his breath back by sitting on the floor. Rogan wasn't one to let people get away with shit like that, but he didn't want to die either. Instead, he just sat there and waited.

"Your sister and brother, they'll come to help you, yes?" Rogan nodded, then shook his head. "Which is it, man? I'm a vampire that is on edge. I do not have time for your bullshit. I'm here because I was called in to help you. Which I do not want to do, but am obligated to."

"Yeah, they're both attorneys, but my sister would just as soon kill me as to help me. She has a burr up her ass." He might have said something like everyone did, but he wasn't sure if he should poke the bear, as his mom used to say. "Tyrrell, he's a good boy. I was gonna call him in a minute or two. You want him here?"

"I don't care who you call, but I want someone to come here and take care of this mess." He asked him his name. "Daegan. I knew your family long ago, and owe them a single favor. Since I have been called in to help, then I have no choice but to do so. Your great grandmother, she was a friend of mine."

Rogan wondered who would have called a vampire in to help him. His grannie had been dead almost since he'd been born. But it mattered little. If this creature was going to help him, then he'd use him.

"Do you know who helped them? My wife and kids?" He said that he didn't yet, but would soon. "You leave them to me. I'll take care of the fuckers."

"You can barely take care of yourself and keep your wife and kids here. How do you expect to take care of someone that has enough power to not only move your family, but her brother as well? You cannot. You're to leave them to me."

Rogan asked him why. "Because the sooner I get this taken care of, the faster I will no longer have a hold over me. Just tell me what you know."

"I don't know shit. I was knocking her around a bit on account'a she got this burr up her ass about something. She was forever pissed off about this or that. Then this guy comes to the door and tells her that he'll run her to the hospital. That her fucking dumbass brother is hurt. What a pussy he is. And you know what, he's queer too." Daegan asked him why that was a problem. "I don't know. Men and men together? Hell, that just ain't right."

"Yes, well, I can see where your opinion would hold a lot of weight. This person that came to your home, how did he get around you if you were only…what did you call it, knocking her around a bit?" Rogan nodded, but he wasn't sure he was really asking him or just making fun. "How did he get her to go with him?"

"He's a big fucker. Bigger than you are. And strong. He just hit me the one time and I went down like a log." Rogan wondered why he was telling the man that; usually it was his habit to make himself look better than he was. "You got some kind of voodoo on you that makes me have to tell you the truth?"

"Yes, that's it. Voodoo. It's all the rage now. Was this man human?" He asked how he could tell. "If he didn't shift or anything else to you, then I'm going to assume that he is anyway. You're a fat fuck, and hitting you once to knock you down wouldn't have been a human's first response."

Again, it was difficult to tell if he was being insulted or what. So he only sat there, thinking of the shit he was going to have to do to get his family back. Daegan started pacing,

178

so to get out of his way, he got up and sat at the dining room table. At the head of it. Even if they weren't there, he needed someone to know that he was in charge.

"Call your brother and tell him you need him." It might be a little more involved than that, he told Daegan. "And why is that? Have you managed to piss off more of your family members?"

"Something like that. I owe him some money. And if nothing else, Tyrrell is a man who likes to keep track of what he owns or someone owes him." Daegan asked him how much he owed. "About five grand."

"Christ." The money appeared on the table, and before he could snatch it up, Daegan smacked his hand. "You use that for anything other than getting your brother to help you, then so help me, I'm going to come back here and fuck you up."

"I'll pay him." Rogan wished now that he'd thought of more money that he owed his brother. That was just too easy. The phone appeared a second later, and he tried to remember his brother's number. When it started to dial it up for him, he thought about having someone around like this vamp all the time. Then Tyrrell answered the phone. "Hey, little brother, it's Rogan. I was wondering if you could come on here and help your big brother out."

"No. I told you before, unless you pay me what you owe me, then you're on your own. I heard from Bridget, by the way. Smart girl, leaving you like that." He told his bother he was getting her back. "Why? Just leave her alone, Rogan. She's a nice woman. Do you want her to end up like Mom? Hating Dad with every breath she took? Just let her live her life and you move on."

"I can't do that. She took my kids." He didn't say anything, so he looked down at the cash. "I have your money right here. All five grand of it."

"I don't believe you." He said that he could take a picture of it and send it to him. "Look, Rogan, why don't you call Giynna? I know that she's on vacation right now. Call her and see if she'll do it. I just don't have time."

"You're my brother, Tyrrell. Come on, help me out. Just this one time." He said that he would. "Thanks so much. I really appreciate—"

"I'll call Giynna. Give her the money. I don't think it's even close to enough to pay her back what you owe her, but use it to soften the blow at you calling her. And Rogan, don't call me again. I won't be dragged down to your level again. I doubt that Giynna will want to help you for the same reasons." Before he could point out again how he was his brother, the line went dead. He looked up at Daegan.

"He's being a shit about this. Like he thinks I'm some sort of lowlife." The vamp asked him if he was. "No. I got me a job when I want one. There are a lot of things I can do too. And if I work too much, those fuckers at the offices downtown, they cut my food card. That just ain't right. When they tell you that you're gonna get this much a month, they can't be taking if from you just on account'a your old lady made you get out and find something useful to do."

"Yes, well, I can see how that would stick in your craw. Imagine that, wanting you to make yourself an upstanding citizen." Again, he wasn't sure that he was making fun at him or not, so he let it go. "Then call your sister. You need to have legal representation, and while I'd love to help you with that, these things are usually conducted during a time when I cannot be out in the sun."

"I can tell you now, she's not going to help me. She might come along and help them burn me, and you too should it come to that. I don't like her much, but she is meaner than a bear that's been poked." Daegan asked him to speak English. "I was. Shit man, ain't you ever heard of not poking the bear?"

"I have, but not like you put it. Call her. Then when this is finished, you can go about your life as you were before." He asked him if he'd get his family back. "I suppose that would depend on how your sister does in the courtroom."

He called but she didn't pick up. Rogan knew that some people wouldn't answer a call that they didn't know. His wife had gotten into the habit of not answering his calls, nor those of bill collectors. And there were a lot of those. Leaving a message for Giynna to call him back, he asked Daegan what he thought was going to happen if nobody came to his rescue.

"You'll go to jail again. This time for a bit longer than just a few days. You violated your order that was put before you several months ago, in that you're not to use your wife as a punching bag." Rogan told him that she begged for it. "Yes, I'm sure that she does. As soon as you come in the door, she's all over you to take a swing at her face. Some women are just too hard to please."

"I don't know if you're insulting me or having fun at me." He said that he was most assuredly insulting him. "Why you wanna go and do that for? I ain't done nothing wrong."

"Just keep calling your sister. And your brother too. One of them has to come to help you, and since I know for a fact that you have no money of your own, nor enough for a retainer, then you'd have to take a court appointed attorney, and that won't get you anything but a longer prison sentence. You need someone that has a vested interest in your wellbeing."

181

Rogan asked him if he thought they'd help. "I don't know because I can well imagine that anyone you come in contact with to even speak to you might have an unnatural urge to keep you behind bars. For life. Or perhaps it is just what you need. But I made a promise and I must keep it."

When the vampire left him, Rogan tried to figure out what the hell his family would have to do with a vampire and why he was going to help him. So far as Rogan could think, he'd done nothing wrong but kept his wife and kids in line. Bridge always was a stickler for making herself the victim when he was pissed with her. And that seemed to be all the time now. She just didn't want to listen to him when he told her something. As he tried to call his sister again, he wondered what was up his brother's butt. Sure, he did owe him money, but that wasn't enough to keep him from coming to help him. At least Rogan didn't think it was. And if Daegan could give him money to pay his brother, why couldn't he pay off some fancy lawyer to come and help him? If he really needed it.

"It sounds to me like he's lazy too. And whatever this problem I have is, which ain't nothing to get all twisted up about, then why don't he just make it go away?" Lots of questions that had no answers. He'd just have to think on it.

Going in the bedroom to take a nap, he realized his mistake as soon as he laid down. The fucking shit that he'd put on the bed was now all over his body. Rogan thought he could hear someone laughing at him, and knew that it was the vampire.

Things had better start going his way or he'd have to take measures. He wasn't clear on what those might be, but someone, namely his wife, was going to get their ass kicked.

As he threw out the sheets and blankets, he tried to make the bed. But since he couldn't remember how to do it, having had Bridget around for that sort of women's work, he showered then laid down. Fucking bitch was going to have a lot to explain when she got back.

~~~

Randal sat at his desk and finished up the paperwork that came with his job. There was a meeting in half an hour, and he thought that going home then coming back would waste more time than he wanted to give it right now. This meeting couldn't have come at a worse time. He wanted to be home, with his wife and his little girl.

When he heard someone open his classroom door, he looked up. Even though the school was in a temporary place, he still got the willies each time there was some sound that he didn't recognize. The shooting and the deaths still weighed heavily on his heart and mind, but he thought he was doing much better. In a few months, less if the town's people had anything to say about it, they'd be in the school again, and classes would, for the most part, be the same.

"I knew I'd find you here." He nodded at the superintendent as he sat in one of the little chairs his class was using. "I need to talk to you before this meeting."

"No." Randal leaned back in his chair. "I'm not going to take the principal job. No matter how many times you ask, the answer is still no."

When his mom and dad came in the room, he stood up. Asking them if everything was all right, he returned his mom's kiss on his cheek and sat down with Mr. Pillar. As soon as his dad sat, he knew that he was being outnumbered.

"Randal, do you have any idea how much this will mend

the communities for you to take this job?" He shook his head. "Don't give me that until you hear me out. This school has seen enough troubles lately. First there was the breakdown in communications that we had with the last school fundraiser. Then there was that idiot that was…he was a monster and we both know it."

"Mom, I really enjoy teaching. If I take this job like everyone thinks I should, then I'll miss that. I love being a teacher." She nodded and looked over at his dad. "Dad?"

"Hey, don't ask me to chime in. I was already told that I was to agree with her or not get any dinner for a week. I don't think she's gonna do that, but you just don't know about women." Mom smacked him upside the head. "Well, that's what you told me. And I have to say I agree with you anyhow. What's the alternative? Let the school pick again? They did such a bang-up job at it the last time. And maybe that once they pick the wrong person for the job, we won't have a school at all around here."

"Dad, you can't do this to me." His dad stood up and handed him a thick notebook. He only glanced at it, knowing what it was. "What does this have to do with me taking this job?"

"Teacher of the year ten years in a row. Ten whole years. Then in there are letters from parents, cards from the kids you taught. I saved every one of them. Articles in the paper. I even put in there your first ID tag that you got when you started teaching. That is all you, son. A man who knows how to be a good leader." He felt his face heat up. Randal looked at Mr. Pillar and asked him again to stop this. "He's not going to. And let me tell you why not. Because when you leave here today, you're going to tell every single person that is in the parking lot right now that you turned this job down."

"What do you mean? The parking lot is full of people?" His mom showed him the picture she'd taken. "I can't believe this."

"Well, you believe it. And that's not all. They have refused to help out with any kind of fundraisers unless you take the job." Blackmail. He was being blackmailed by the entire town. When Trent and the rest of his brothers joined them in his classroom, he gave up. "Well, son? What's it going to be?"

"You've left me no choice in the matter, haven't you? I'm taking the job, but I'm not going to be happy with it." Mr. Pillar left them, but his family sat around the little tables. "I hope you're happy with this. I've just taken a job that I don't want."

Trent stood up and cleared his throat. When he started speaking, Randal thought for sure that someone was forcing him to do this, but Trent assured him that he was on his own and that, unlike him, was excited.

"I'm going to come in and teach twice a week. Reading. And not only that, but I've been made part of the football team coaching staff so that I can help there as well." Trent looked at Sterl, who stood up.

"I'm coming in once a week, when I don't have anything going on, and help out with the art classes. Also, I've donated funds so that they can have the kind of supplies to encourage young minds to pursue something that they want." Sterl laughed. "And then at the end of the school year, I'm going to display all the artwork in the gallery. I'm hoping to make it a yearly event."

Scott was going to come in and teach self-defense classes. Also to talk about safe sex and other things. Chloe was going to help him with that. Elijah volunteered to come in twice a month to go over some of the things that they might find useful in the world. Like how to get out of a burning house, who to go to when things were bad at home. And how to use a cellphone. Tanner was going to show the older kids how to use a credit card safely, fill out a check, as well as a bank record.

"And this is because I'm taking the job?" They all nodded, and Trent told him that he would have to approve all this but they'd help out. "All right, I can see this working. But you do know that the board has to approve any and all of you working here."

"That would be myself and your mom. We've taken over the board, so to speak. Also, we've approved a fundraiser, which your wife is working on, to have food here at the school for kids to take home should they need it. There is also going to be a before and after school place for kids to come when their parents are at work. A place they can have a quick snack, as well as some activities they can do before going home." Randal thanked his mom. "Don't just thank me. This is all of them. Sterl organized his brothers and found out what they could do to help you. And the added bonus for all of them and for you is to get to be together."

He was overwhelmed by the support that he was getting. And not only that, that his brothers were so willing to come in and help out. That alone would help a great many people. He looked down at the note that he'd gotten today and decided to share it with them.

"Doug sent me this this morning. It says that he'll be hiring another two hundred people by spring. And he is willing to donate a lot of computers to the schools. That will be a dozen computers for each level of education." They all cheered. "And he promised to help any other businesses coming in too, so that they don't have as many start up issues as he had."

"See what I mean, son? You're good for this place. I don't mean that you had anything to do with the hiring and computers, but just you being the principal is gonna help out in ways that we can't even begin to see right now." He told his dad that he doubted very much he was going to be any good at the job. "Well, I don't want to be crude here, but I know for a fact that you're not going to be hurting anyone here. And that to me is the great thing."

When the board meeting began, his family was right there with him when Mr. Pillar announced that Randal was going to take the job. He could almost feel the excitement in the room. It seemed that his parents were right...they might have quit had he not taken over the job. But to do this, he had to make some major changes in his life. And that wasn't even counting finding someone to take his job as the kindergarten teacher.

After the meeting he made his way home. He was going to work until the end of the school year as both principal and part time teacher. It was going to be hard on him, lots of time spent away from his home and family, but Laney told him that she'd help in any way that she could. Even Wally said he'd put in a helping hand when he'd let him. With so much support, Randal was sure he could make it work.

"Dad, did you know that Mrs. Walden is retiring soon? She said that we're too much for her." He asked her when she'd said that. "Yesterday when some of the kids threw spit balls at her. You know what, that's discussing." He told her it was disgusting, not discussing. "Yeah, that's what I meant. Anyway, she said that she can't take it no more."

"Anymore, and I'm sorry to hear that." He wasn't, but he'd never tell a child that. Mrs. Walden had been his teacher when he was a child. And she was the most brutal, mean, sarcastic teacher he'd ever had the misfortune of working with. She hated change, even to bring computers into her classroom. He was glad to see her go on her own, because he would have had to fire her.

That reminded him that he had a lot of work to catch up on with finding replacements. As of today he had to find two teachers, plus a secretary for him. They'd lost one when the school had been shot up, and he dreaded having to find someone else.

Just as he was going up to bed with Laney, he remembered something that his mom had told him. That someone needed to be working that job that had a good eye for people. He thought they'd be better off finding someone that had military background, just to make sure that the kids stayed in line and safe and no one could just come in and hurt any of them. Smiling, he told Laney what he was thinking.

"Maybe we should hire pack for that job. I mean, they can sniff out trouble as fast as you can." He thought that had merit. "Also, they can heal faster should there be a flu or something. That way you'd not have to run that place on your own. Something that I'd run from as fast and as far as I can."

CHAPTER 13

Chris Bentley knew that she was doing wrong, but there wasn't any other way. Rogan was supposed to have been dead by now. Not by her hand, though there were enough times that she wished she had done it. Now, because he'd made such enemies of his siblings, the young woman might not come to Tanner. And that was something that needed to happen. She paced her office until Myra told her to please sit down.

"And what if she doesn't come around? We're all going to be fucked if she decides he's not worth it." Myra said she'd come. "Why? I'd not. He's a prick that should have his balls cut off, and him made to eat them."

"Such violence. She'll come, and once she's here, all will fall into place. You said that yourself." She nodded. "Why do you think we're going to be fucked? A word, I might add, I still do not understand."

"It means, in this case, to be screwed. And we won't, not really. Poor Tanner will be. He's going to need his mate to be happy. And we know that happiness is what I strive for." Myra snorted. "You don't think that's what I want for everyone?"

"I think that you are smitten with the young man. Not in love with him of course, but you do love him a tad more than the rest of them." She did admit that. "And he's got a piece of my heart too. Oh, before I forget, he can sire children now. He asked me to fix things in his house for his mate, so since he was in there, I took it upon myself to fix him as well. Sneaky yes, but it was something that I needed to do for him."

"Thank you." Myra waved her off. "Where is Daegan? I would have thought he'd of been there and back by now. He was supposed to return here, correct?"

"Yes, well, I told you not to hire him. I know that he wanted to do this for you, and the reward that you offered him should he make it happen is great, but he isn't the smartest of the lot." Chris just smiled. "This woman, Giynna, you know what her name means?"

"Yes, of the glen. I think that it fitting, don't you? That she will be someone to come to the family that will spice things up?" Myra said they had a great deal of spice now. "Yes, but Giynna is so.... She takes the term fiery redhead to the highest levels. The perfect person for our young Tanner."

Chris loved the Calhouns. They were a group of wolves that she had come to love and called friends. They had treated her and her family with respect, and had, at one time, called them to help in a way that had not just saved them, but her family as well. Helenia, the she-devil, would have harmed her family too had she not been dealt with when she had. And that, as far as Chris was concerned, was enough for her to be indebted to the Calhoun family forever.

An hour later, Daegan showed up. He told them that he

was sorry that he'd taken so long, but he had one thing that he wished to look at before he came back. He wished to see the ocean and the boats that rode upon it.

"The ocean is a beautiful thing. You should have called me to let me know that you were running late. I've worried about you." He said something as he knelt before her, and Chris asked him to repeat it.

"I said that I was afraid if I called you, you would have summoned me back and I would not have been able to see such a sight, my lady." Chris looked at Myra, who pouted. The young faerie had asked to be let go from his services with her and his own queen. He didn't want to live any longer, it seemed. "It was my last thing I wished to do. I do ask your forgiveness, my lady, but as you told us before, we were to take chances."

"Yes, I did. And since you have done as I have asked so well, I shall grant you your wish. You are ready to receive it." He said that he had said his goodbyes and had gotten his things together. "Very well. You are no longer in my service as a faerie."

He stiffened…she could see it in the line of his body. And when he peeked up at her, looking with one eye closed, she nearly laughed. It wasn't what he had thought he was getting, but so much more.

"My lady?" She asked him to stand. "I don't know what is going on. You were to remove my head, correct?"

"No. I said you could be out of my service. I don't know what you thought was going to happen. But you're a good man, and I do hate to have good men killed just because they want to see the world. You will retain some of your magic. Your queen has also asked that you come to see her before you leave, if you wish. She would like to ask another favor of you. Since you are human looking now, you can help us both a great deal." He stood up and touched his fingers to his face and body. "You're happy?"

"Yes. I never...did you know this before I left you?" She said that she'd talked to the queen of faeries before he had left to do her service. "And what would you have done had I not returned?"

"It's not in you to disobey a command nor a favor. That's why we decided to grant you your fondest wish. To live among the humans as one." He giggled, then covered his mouth. "You're happy, and you should be. This is something that the queen and I worked on together. And hopefully, when we need you and you're not busy, you can help us again."

"I shall. You have only to ask." He did a little jig in the middle of the room, and she laughed with him. "I am a man. A man that can do as he wishes."

"You are. And I thank you for your help with this." He bent before her again and she let him kiss her hand. It was one of the hardest things that she had to get used to, people treating her like she was important. "Go on now, talk to the queen. And before I forget, Myra has a place for you to stay while you figure things out, as well as some cash. My family will help you for a little while, just to get used to spending money and working, so heed what they tell you."

When he was gone, she sat down. There wasn't much left for her to do now but to wait. Myra said that she'd go see the woman, just to check her out in a couple of days. It was basically in Giynna's hands now.

There wasn't much to do now that she had her house in order. Not just her home, but her job too, being the queen of witches, the grand witch, she could pretty much do as she wished and make it happen. But the fun of that had gone out a few years ago. Now she did things because she wanted. So long as she followed the rules. And there were a great many of them.

"Myra, I need a vacation." She just smiled at her. "You know where I should be going? I was thinking France. Just to see the spring. Joseph and I need to get away, more than ever I think."

"You don't wish to go to Ireland?" She shook her head. "You could see the worth of the woman who will save the Calhoun family. It might be nice to be prepared."

"No. I don't want to get any more involved than I already am. And that's a great deal more than I should have been." Myra said nothing. "I don't want them harmed in anything, but this, this brother of theirs, he's going to cause trouble even I don't know how to fix."

"But you could, should you wish it." She nodded and thought about the vacation. "You're really not going?"

"No, I'm really not. You go and take care that she goes to Ohio, but the rest of it, I have done all that I can for them." Myra said that she had. "Good, then we're in agreement. You will see to her, and I'll go away for a week or so. I can take care of most things that come up, and if they do, I can just pop in and out to fix it. I'll have fun."

"You sound as if you're trying to convince yourself." Chris huffed at her. "I think you are a wonderful person, and the best grand witch the world has ever known. You go, have some fun, and when you return, we'll work on a couple of other things. Also, you should know that Sterl has agreed to paint the family for you. I think it will make a great gift to them."

"Yes, I was thinking that too. Joseph's family has been the best to me." They all had too. As she closed her eyes, thinking that a short nap was in order, she thought of her involvement in the Calhoun family. "I think in the spring we should have a picnic. After the babies are born there. And invite the Calhouns here. To do something together that has nothing to do with magic or with trouble would be a nice change."

She was getting sleepier, and she had a feeling that Myra had something to do with her sudden need to go into a deeper sleep. But asking her seemed too much trouble, so she let it take her under. She'd been very tired a lot lately.

~~~

Giynna eyed her phone. It had done nothing but ring off the hook for several hours now. And she was ready to answer it when it rang again, but this time her other brother's face popping up. Snatching the phone up, she answered with a less than nice greeting. His laughter made her smile.

"Yes, it's me, and I do have something fucking going on. Does your boss know you talk like that?" She said that he was the one that taught her. "Ah, so it's a good thing. I called to let you know that Rogan is in trouble again. And that Bridget has left him."

"Good for her. What's he done now? Please tell me that he didn't kill her brother. I liked Phillip." He said he did too, but he was not dead. "What has he done now? I'm assuming that he called you first."

Her phone was telling her that she had another call which, like the others, she ignored. Making a mark on her pad of paper, she counted that he'd called her fifty-four times since last night.

"Apparently Bridget had taken a restraining order out against him, and when he broke into the house, someone came along and beat the shit out of him when he wouldn't let her leave. Phillip was injured on the job. I guess he's left the area too." She leaned back in her chair and thought of all the shit her brother Rogan had gotten into since he'd been born. Probably even before that, if it was possible. "He needs one of us to go there as his attorney."

"No. I'm assuming, since you've called me, that he asked you first." He said that he had. "I'm not going to help him again. I'm finished with his ass and stupidity."

"Yes, but I have a plan, if you'll listen." She told him to go ahead, but she wasn't budging on this one. "How about we go there together? It would be a nice way for us to see each other again. And deal with him as a pair. Plus, I've been playing around with a contract too, one that he'll sign or we'll never talk to him again. I doubt it'll work, but I promise you, if you go there to help me, we'll deal with him calmly. And you know as well as I do that we do better when we have each other's backs."

"You're making this very hard, Tyrrell. I have a life here, one that I like very much. My house isn't flawless, which is doubtful I can ever make that work. So I've come to terms with its never going to be exactly what I want. But to go there and help him, it goes against everything inside of me. I hate to say this, but he needs to be put in prison and never thought of again." He told her that he really missed her. "And you think we'll get to visit all that much with him fucking around with us?"

"Yes, I do. We'll make sure of it. And while you're in the States, we'll head to wherever Bridget is. Wouldn't it be nice

195

to see the kids again too?" She looked over at the gifts that she had for them but hadn't sent. Simply because she knew that Rogan would tear them up or sell them. "Come on, you know that you want to."

"All right, damn it. I'll go, but you had better be thinking of someplace really nice to take me out to dinner. And I don't mean that place you love. I want more than just French fries and a burger. Or else." He laughed and said it was a deal. "And you're paying for half my ticket and all my bail money if I have to murder him."

"Deal." He agreed too quickly, and she asked him what was up. "Nothing. I'm just excited to see you again. It's been a long time."

"It has. And while I don't relish the fact that we're going to work with him, I am looking forward to hanging out with my favorite brother." And he was, since the first time and the last time that Rogan hit her hard enough to knock her out, as well as rob her. She'd never forgive him for that, and she didn't think that he cared. "I'll make arrangements and then call you. Do you know of any hotels there in the area?"

"I'll set us both up a place. I'm so glad that you're coming, Giynna. I've missed you a great deal." She told him she was as well and hung up. In a few hours she'd be able to call her boss, but didn't know what to tell him. Giynna hated to miss work, even if she was using her vacation time. And she had a lot of it.

By the time she was ready to call her boss and tell him that she had a family emergency, she was not only packed up but she'd made arrangements to fly, gotten her passport ready, and found a box big enough to send the gifts to Bridget and the kids. Tyrrell had called her back, not only with an address for their sister-in-law, but also the name of the hotel, and told her a car was going to pick her up. She was as set as she'd ever be, she supposed. But she still wasn't looking forward to seeing Rogan.

When she'd been seventeen he'd found her hiding place. Her mother was still alive then, and she had put up with his abuse too before just leaving them. Their father, a man that was more absent than there, hadn't done anything to keep him from hurting any of them, so she had decided that she was old enough to get out on her own. She only wished that she'd done it earlier instead of waiting for her graduation from high school to move.

"Give me some money." She'd told Rogan that she didn't have any to give him. "Which means you have it, you're just not willing to share it. That's not fair, Ginny."

He called her that because she hated it, but this time she didn't let him see her hatred. Turning her back on him, she was only two steps from the door when he hit her. Pain exploded in the back of her head and she went down.

Blood ran down her back as he jerked her up from the floor. She puked on him; the pain was too much for her. And when he tossed her across the room, letting her hit not just the wall behind her but the table and chairs as well, the leg of the chair broke off and entered her leg just below her knee. Screaming now, she knew that he was going to kill her.

Picking up her purse, he took out her wallet and tossed the rest at her. He took her money, all one hundred dollars of the cash that she had in it. Holding the purse to her chest, she screamed at him to give it to her when he stood over her, his fist doubled up.

"Hit her and I'll kill you." She looked at Tyrell and begged him to go away. That was when she saw the gun. "Rogan, you touch her again and I will kill your fucking ass."

Rogan threw her wallet at her and left them. But he hit Tyrrell too, knocking him out before he could come to her. She could still hear his laughter; Rogan's laugh was much like a braying jackass, and she knew that it would haunt her for years to come.

The neighbor who heard the noise had called the police. Rogan would be arrested, they knew that, and it would give them both time to get away. And because she'd planted the money for him to find, she still had enough left to get herself a ticket and go stay with her grandma in Ireland. As soon as she was released from the hospital, she took the very next flight out and never returned. But she would now, to see her brother again and hopefully make sure that Rogan was put away for a very long time.

~~~

Myra put the phone back in the cradle and knew that soon she'd have to go and talk to young Tyrrell. He would have to play along with her plan or his sister would be mad. Well, madder. Pretending to be the man had worked out better than she could have hoped. Not only was she coming to Ohio, but she was going to be mated to the best man she could ever have chosen for her.

Smiling, she pulled her clothing around her to suit her mood and laughed. Balloons were her favorite, and she loved that they were all over her dress. As she made her way to her room, the place where she did her own conjuring, she thought about the bastard Rogan.

Had she known beforehand what he'd done to his siblings, she might have handled things differently. But it was set now, and she was going to keep an eye on them both. There wasn't any reason to believe that once she came to meet Tanner that she'd be safe. It was what she was counting on too. But still, she wanted to make sure that everything was going to go well for them, so she pulled out her book.

It was well after midnight when she had things the way she wanted them. And her conversation with Tyrrell had gone well too. He would do as she asked, for the simple reason he wanted to see his sister as well. Myra was going to take a long vacation herself when this was done. She had no idea where she'd go, but it would be a long one. Laughing, she wondered what on earth she could do after living so many years.

"I'll find something."

She would too. Perhaps make a little trouble for herself too. When she went to her bedroom to read, she wondered, not for the first time, what she'd have done with her life had Chris not needed her. Or the Calhouns. Life, she knew, had been pretty boring, and she was glad for their company.

Before You Go...

HELP AN AUTHOR

write a review

THANK YOU!

Share your voice and help guide other readers to these wonderful books. Even if it's only a line or two your reviews help readers discover the author's books so they can continue creating stories that you'll love. Login to your favorite retailer and leave a review. Thank you.

AWARD WINNING, BESTSELLING AUTHOR

Kathi Barton, winner of the Pinnacle Book Achievement award as well as a best-selling author on Amazon and All Romance books, lives in Nashport, Ohio with her husband Paul. When not creating new worlds and romance, Kathi and her husband enjoy camping and going to auctions. She can also be seen at county fairs with her husband who is an artist and potter.

Her muse, a cross between Jimmy Stewart and Hugh Jackman, brings her stories to life for her readers in a way that has them coming back time and again for more. Her favorite genre is paranormal romance with a great deal of spice. You can visit Kathi online and drop her an email if you'd like. She loves hearing from her fans. aaronskiss@gmail.com.

Follow Kathi on her blog: http://kathisbartonauthor.blogspot.com/

www.ingramcontent.com/pod-product-compliance
Lightning Source LLC
Chambersburg PA
CBHW032130170626
46808CB00006B/2179